Totally *Unexpected!*

First Edition

Published by The Nazca Plains Corporation
Las Vegas, Nevada
2010

ISBN: 978-1-935509-27-1

Published by

The Nazca Plains Corporation ®
4640 Paradise Rd, Suite 141
Las Vegas NV 89109-8000

PUBLISHER'S NOTE
Totally Unexpected! is a work of fiction created wholly by *Wade
Wright's* imagination. All characters are fictional and any resemblance
to any persons living or deceased is purely by accident. No portion
of this book reflects any real person or events.

Cover Male Photo, newphotoservice
Art Director, Blake Stephens

DEDICATION

To each individual that has discovered life does have its varieties
and its surprises, and manages to accept those unexpected elements
as part of our joys of living!

Totally *Unexpected!*

First Edition

Wade Wright

CONTENTS

AT THE BACK DOOR, NAKED

On the phone, Shane was talking to a rather newfound friend from the bathhouse. Shane was a 29 year old farm boy – or if you prefer, a rather spoiled 29 year old, big plantation family offspring, since the farm was now much more of a local landmark than a working farm. The acreage was now all leased out to other farmers in the area, but the house and all of the out buildings, such as the old horse and buggy barn, still remained.

Although the Hargrove family no longer did any of the active farming, the family as a whole, four brothers and one sister, did want to keep the property up and in good repair, since they did feel that as the years moved on it could become a very valuable piece of property and history in the area. Shane and his wife Barbara lived on the property and as their share of maintaining the property Shane did all of the repairs, painting and other upkeep.

"Hey, Tab – look. Barbara took the kids over to Brooksville to see their Grandma and Grandpa, and she's gonna be gone until at least six or seven tonight. Come on over here, and let's play here. This place is way back off of the road, real private, and we can do some of our naked stuff outside if we want to. Hey, we can go out and do some sucking and fucking in one of the old barns if we want! – No, no! Just you and me! Hey, everybody else's gotta be at work today. We'll have the entire afternoon all to ourselves and we can do whatever, wherever we want. Okay? – Yeah, okay. Hey, Tab! When you come out here, come back the drive, park back by the old farm wagon back there and strip naked before you come to the back door. I wanna see that fucking big long piece of meat swinging in front of you, when you come in the house! – Hey, don't worry. When you get here you'll see how far off of the road it is and how private it is. Nobody's gonna see that hot tight ass of yours 'cept me, and I'm getting pretty damn anxious for it again! It's gonna be just you and me, and we can have a better time here than at the bathhouse. Okay? – Yeah, of course I'll be naked! Gotta show what I bring to the party too, ya know! Okay, see you then in about half an hour! Bye man, and – bring it hard!"

Tab was a couple of years older than Shane, and maybe about twenty to twenty-five pounds heavier. Shane stood right at six foot one, and weighed in at 195. He had definitely thrown his share of hay bales in his younger days – as his thick deep chest and his 18-inch biceps showed.

Tab was just about the same height, but as discovered in the locker room at the bathhouse about a week earlier, he did outweigh Shane by about twenty-three pounds. Of course Shane's comment at that time was, "Well hell man! If I was swinging as much meat between my legs as you are, I'd weigh that much too! How long is that fucker anyway?"

"Hell man, it ain't that fucking big! Shit man, it's only about two inches longer than yours, and when yours gets hard, I sure as hell ain't gonna compare mine with yours any! Yours must get about as big around as some fucking beer can when it's hard, and no black man's gonna have some white guy's dick showing up bigger than his own! So when I fuck the hell out of that ass of yours, you just be glad it's as long as it is, cause the way you and your ass eats it up, you'd probably take another nine or ten inches if I had it!"

Running for the back door as Shane heard the car door slam shut, he rounded the corner of the kitchen and headed into the "mudroom" and threw open the door.

Of course, as he had told Tab he'd be, he threw open the back door, and was now standing at the back door, fully and totally naked.

"Shane, what the hell!?

"Oh, shit, man, I thought it was somebody else. I mean – uh, Clay – let me grab some shorts – let me grab some shorts!"

True, there was a car out back, and a man at the door, and right at about the same time that Tab was supposed to be there, but this was no Tab! It was brother Clay!

Coming in the door and watching his kid brother scurry across the kitchen – bare assed as a guy can be, Clay emphatically asked, "Shane, you thought it was somebody else!? What in the hell is going on here that you'd come to the door, bare as hell, thinking it was somebody else!? Who in the hell!? What in the hell is going on here? Shane, what's going on?"

As Shane grabbed a pair of cutoffs and pulled 'em on, he looked at his brother with a very, very concerned look on his face. Not only had he really screwed up in front of his brother, but now Tab was expected to show up at any minute, and if he follows the earlier orders, he's gonna be coming in all bare assed and swinging too!

"Shane, Shane, explain to me, just what in the hell is going on? I really don't understand."

Just as Clay was really emphatically asking for an explanation – of course – right then, Tab pulled in. He immediately stripped off the only thing he had on – a pair of shorts – and as he had been told to do, he got out of the car and headed for the back door.

Shane heard the car door, and he looked toward the back door; Clay did likewise.

There was a light tap on the door. Clay looked at Shane and asked, "Well, you gonna go answer the door?"

Knowing just what was about to happen, Shane took a very deep breath, and moving past Clay, he headed for the door.

Clay opened the door, Tab looked at him and said, "Hey, man! Thought you were gonna be hanging it and swinging it too! What's up, why the pants?"

Just as Tab asked, Clay came around the corner, and of course took a big long look at the hunk of walnut brown meat that was now standing there, showing it all, including a ten-inch hard-on.

"Oh, shit, man, what in the fuck is going on here man? Shane, who in the hell is this, and just what in the hell is going on here?" Then turning and looking at this brother, Clay said. "First you're naked, going to the door naked and telling me you thought I was someone else, now he comes in, completely naked, and of course with a fucking hard-on showing! Shane, just what in the hell is going on? Shane, you and this guy doing something? Seriously man, what in the hell is going on here? You guys playing or something?"

With Tab now standing there quite nervously but not saying anything, Shane finally said, "Tab, this is my brother Clay. I did not know he was gonna be coming by here. I'm sorry, I didn't know it."

Clay looked at Tab, and kinda of in a very, very small way, he nodded as if to be saying "Hi."

Tab looked at Clay, and did say, "Hi." He then looked back at Shane as if to ask, "What's up? What's up? We got trouble?"

Looking at Clay, Shane finally said, "Clay, Tab and I are friends, and we met a few weeks ago at a bathhouse. Clay, he and I play around. I sure as hell didn't expect anybody to come here today, and I asked him to come over here. Yeah, Clay, yeah – I play with guys."

Tab took a very deep breath, looked at Shane with a big amount of concern, and then quickly over toward Clay with even a bigger amount of not only concern, but maybe some fear as well.

Stunned and shocked, Clay did not say anything right away, but he did look at his brother, eyeball-to-eyeball, and then over to Tab, but that was not eyeball-to-eyeball. That was much more the head to toe, and a slight pause at the still hard ten inches of meat, sticking out like a tree that had fallen over.

Looking back at his brother, Clay then asked, "Shane, does Barbara know about this? How long's this been going on?"

Nervous and scared as hell, Shane timidly looked at Clay and replied, "No, hell no, she don't know! God Clay, don't tell her! Don't tell anybody!"

"Shane I won't, I won't! Seriously man, I won't! How long you been doing this stuff?"

"I've been doing it since I was in high school. Jimmy and I did it all the time, man – every time we could – we did it. That's why he moved to Chicago. He's got a partner now. He's an open gay guy up there. I don't do it very often, but Tab and I met and Clay – look at him! He's hot and yeah, I like doing stuff with him. Please, don't blame him any for being here or being naked or anything – it was all my doings. When I called him and asked if he could come out here today, I was the one that told him to take everything off before he came to the door. Yeah – that's why I was naked when you got here. I thought it was him coming in. I sure as hell did not expect you or anybody else to show up here today! Clay, Clay, what can I say? Please, don't tell Barbara or anybody else, please, please!"

"Hey, Shane, Shane, calm down, I'm not gonna! I won't, seriously man, I won't!" Then, very calmly and reassuringly, he added, "I've done if before too. I think all guys do or have at some time."

Shocked and surprised, Shane looked at his older brother and asked, "You have!? You serious man, you have?"

Then answering Shane, but looking over at Tab, he answered, "Yeah, yeah, but gotta admit – never with something that looks like this one does." Then looking back at this brother, he asked, "What in the hell do you two do together? Look at the dick on that guy! What in the hell do you do with that thing!?"

As Tab stood there, nervous as hell, but still maintaining his composure, as well as his hard-on, and in his thoughts – all due to the unexpected and rather unusual circumstances that he was now involved in, he'd never before been in a situation where he was talked about by two other people, as he just stood there and displayed his ten inches of steel brown rod, with its sack of walnuts hanging down from under it, and its golf ball head showing off just as well. It did have a tip of "shiny" showing right on the tip of it, also. Tab definitely did have reasons to be holding a hard-on!

"Clay, you serious man!? You serious? When? When did you do it? When?"

"I was in the Navy, man – the Navy! Don't think all those neat looking Navy guys walking around in their nice and neat whites are always in the full dress. Let's face it man, servicemen, all branches, they get horny just like civvies do. But like I said, never with some hunk of a man like you found! For a little brother that I always thought did everything wrong, you sure as hell did this one right! Shane, tell me, man – what in the hell do you do with him, and that thing of his? Seriously, you suck on that, get fucked by that, what in the hell do you do?"

Without hesitation, Tab looked at Clay and said, "I fuck him man! I fuck him! He might be your little brother that can't do anything right, but somebody sure as hell taught him how to get it in the ass, and yeah, he does it good!"

Shocked that Tab had entered in the conversation, Shane looked at him and said, "Tab, Tab, please man, please!"

"No man! He asked what we did, and I told him. He must think you don't know how to do stuff right. Well, I want him to know you sure as hell know how to do that, and do it good! And if he wants to see just what it takes to do it good, all he needs to do is drop those pants and I'll give him a first hand chance to see if he can do it too!"

"Hey, I've been fucked before man, I know what it feels like! Yeah, maybe it wasn't that fucking big, but yeah, I've had some black dick up in my ass before, and if you're gonna be nasty and act like I can't take it, just keep it hard!"

All of a sudden, Shane realized that Clay was not acting mad, not at all, but much more over on the "tease me, man, and I'll just show you what I can do, and I'm ready to do it." Shane looked down and realized that his brother was actually rubbing his crotch, and his crotch was showing a tent. All of a sudden, Shane was losing his fear of what the afternoon had turned into, and moving over toward an event where things just might be turning out alright – maybe even to the good!

Quickly looking back and forth between both Clay and Tab, Shane finally asked, "Clay, you want him to fuck you? Do you?"

With a very big grin on his face, Clay replied, "Hell yeah, man, hell yeah! Last time I got it in the ass – what, about ten years ago, and yeah, in San Fran the night before I headed home. I will now admit it, I've missed that hot dick a lot! He was a black man, named Nicky, for Nicholas I think, and every night for a solid week before I shipped home, he did me and I took him for an hour at a time. Yeah, man, yeah! Yeah, I want him to fuck me, and I also wanna watch him fuck you to see just who takes it the fastest! But little brother, you gotta remember it's been about ten years since I've been butt fucked, so I might need to get used to it again. And – especially after seeing that enormous thing sticking out at us! How in the hell did you ever have the nerve the first time, to let him aim that thing at your butt?"

"Wow, shit! Man, I can't believe this! Clay, you serious man, you serious?"

Looking at Shane, grinning, then looking at Tab, still grinning, and then of course down at Tab's rod, Clay responded, "Hell yes man, hell yes! Ten years, and my ass is hungry. Today's turning out a hell of a lot better than it was earlier, a hell of a lot better."

Then looking at his brother with a question mark on his face, Shane asked, "Why? Why? What was wrong? Why did you come out here today anyway? What's up?"

"Oh, hey, man, nothing much. I just came out here today to get you to drive the truck over to the garage for me. Think the tran is going out on it, but hell, man, we can do that tomorrow. Better – much more important things to do today! Come on! Hey, where you gonna play at brother?"

Now with all three men grinning in a big way, Clay and Shane agreed that using the playroom down in the basement of the house might be the most fun place, and after heading down the stairs and into the rec-room, Clay also stripped down, and let not only his younger brother check him out, but his new friend Tab, also.

"Been years and years since I've seen you all bare and naked like that man! Clay, you're looking good, damn good! For an old fart, you've still got it!"

"Hey, little brother! None of the old fart stuff, okay? Remember you're only a couple of years younger, but maybe those two years paid off, cause look at what you found around town, to bring home! I gotta admit, and I think Tab'll agree, you're a pretty hot looking little shit too. Right Tab?"

"Hell yeah, man – hell yeah! And he loves to have that cute little tight bubbled ass of his fucked and fucked good! And of course, guys with dicks like mine, we love to fuck an ass like that! We love it! Down, and in, all the way!"

Clay was the older brother, but only by about three years. He was 32, also a very well built former farm boy that had done his amount of hay bale tossing, but was now a manager for a farm equipment company in town. Six foot even, 220 pounds of solid meat, and of course the traditional Hargrove sliver of fine hair sliding down his chest from just under the Adams apple, into and back out of again, the belly button, and then on down to the top of his more private areas.

Tab reached out, pulled a couple of finger tips of the chest hair out, and said, "Kinda looks like kid brother took after the older brother as far as the hot looking chest hair goes, don't it?" He then, leaned over, took Clay's left tit in his mouth, and slightly sucked on it.

Clay moaned an acceptance and a pleasure. "Sure ain't had that done to those tits in years, thanks man, feels good!" Grinning widely, definitely showing that there were no lingering bad feelings about finding his brother and this man together – well almost together – and about to do some funny gay stuff, Clay replied, "Hey, man! None of the old man stuff, okay!? He and I have two older brothers that we refer to as the old men in the family, so be aware, you're playing with the younger set of the family!"

"Hey, let me tell you guys something!" Tab stated. "I don't care if you're the older set or the younger set, I'm game for both of you, and Clay, if you can take it like your kid brother can, then maybe I can be a good stand-in for your ole Navy buddy, Nicky! Shane, give me some of that grease you've got over there. If it's been ten years since this butt hole's been opened up from the outside, then we just might need to do some finger fucking up in here first. Want that, Clay? Want some fingers up in there?"

Clay laid down on the thick and fuzzy throw rug that was on the floor, and Tab got on top. Not only did he get on top, but then Shane got on top of him. With one white man on the bottom, the brown man in the middle and the other white man now on top, it could have easily been referred to as the roast beef sandwich. Only problem there is, all three pieces of this sandwich were definitely beef, and with the way the top two were, humping, jumping and fucking around – Tab in Clay, and Shane in Tab – there is no way any sandwich could have stayed together for the hour they used each other.

"Oh, man alive!" Clay expounded as he felt the entire length and girth of Tab go in and then sink to the bottom. "Love it man, love it! Oh, Tab, fuck me, man, fuck me! Yeah, you feel just like my buddy Nick did! Damn I loved to be fucked by him! Shit man, I've been needing this, I really have. God, I should have found me a man years ago!"

Then attempting to turn his head back toward both of the men that were on top of him, Clay asked, "Tab, you a local man? You somebody that's gonna be around town for some time?"

"Oh, hell yeah, man, hell yeah! I will admit, I was planning on moving to the St. Louis area sometime soon, but I'm starting to rethink that move. Here I am fucking one of the hottest asses this side of the Mississippi, and right now, while I'm fucking that ass, I've got one of the hottest and thickest dicks around, stuck up in my ass at the same time! So why in the hell would I wanna leave someplace where I can get what I'm getting right now? Yeah, if you two'll promise that we can do stuff like this every once in awhile, like at least twice a month or more, I'll stay around here. St. Louis might have a lot of gays, but right now, I'm not so sure any of 'em can be better than the two straight daddies that I'm with right now! Hang on Clay – hang on! You're about to get a butt full of black man cum up in your ass, hang on! Oh, man, yeah, oh yeah! Oh, Clay, squeeze your ass, squeeze your ass, squeeze your ass!! Oh, shit, man, oh my gawd! Oh, man, I can't believe this, I can't! Yeah, man, yeah! Oh, man! Oh, wow, wow – I can't believe this!"

As Tab was dumping a big hot load up in Clay's ass, which Clay could tell had to be a big load, and he could tell it was all hot, he attempted to ask Tab if he was all right.

"Oh, man, alive, you will not believe this! Oh, man, he shot off in me right at the very same time I was dumping my load right in your ass! Right at the same time! Oh, Clay, I kinda think maybe your kid brother was trying to pass on some family cum on to you, right through me! Shit man, I'm not sure I've ever had some guy shoot off in my ass, right at the very same moment I was cumming in some other guy's ass! Wow! Oh, shit, man! That was without doubt, the best fucking, and getting fucked, at the same time, that I've ever had! Clay, you can take it! You just proved it! I kinda guess your buddy Nick taught you how and taught you well!"

"Yeah, I guess maybe he did! But, part of our deal today was I get fucked, and then I wanna watch you fuck my kid brother so I can see just who can take it the fastest, the hardest and the deepest! So, let's switch this stack around some. You get up on top of him, you fuck him – and while you're fucking him, I'm gonna fuck you and load you and that hot looking bubble butt of yours with some more Hargrove family cum. I ain't cum in some hot tight muscled ass in years! I'm ready to dump my hot load of cum right up in you man – and believe me – I've got a load just waiting to explode!"

And as Clay climbed up on top of Tab's hot looking, solid feeling, tight, sweet little ass, he emphatically stated, "Damn, I'm fucking glad the transmission is going out on my truck!"

TOTALLY CONFUSED

Jimmy Watt, a twenty eight year old former football player (in high school and college), and a neighborhood friend, Stan Bendley, another former football player, when back in school, and about three years behind Jimmy, were on a week-end "football" trip to LA to watch Jimmy's alma mater play Southern Cal. The game had not turned out to be nearly as exciting as had been expected, a really lopsided score, but not Southern Cal's defeat! So anyway, Jimmy was not feeling like the greatest person on the face of the earth, since his week-end was not containing the victory celebration that he was so sure would happen. After the losing game, the two found a nice quiet "out of the way" restaurant, had some rather quiet eating, and some very timid conversation. Jimmy just was not in the mood for being bright and happy!

After the dinner, Stan and Jimmy decided to go back to the hotel for a while, refresh themselves, and rather 'hit the town' in an attempt to lift Jimmy's spirits some and try to get his mind off of the game. The bad score of the game!

With Jimmy standing in the bathroom, shaving – fully naked and bare assed – suddenly the door came open and Stan came in saying, "Hey, I just wanna grab some stuff from the shelf here."

Stan wore only a bath towel wrapped around his waist. Other than the towel, he too was naked and completely bare assed! He had taken his shower just before Jimmy used the bathroom.

Rather surprised and somewhat shocked that Stan had not bothered to knock or even ask if he could come in, Jimmy continued to shave as he noticed that Stan was reaching around his back, to his right side and placing a hand on the counter edge, as he was then reaching up to his left removing a bottle of hand cream that was over toward the left hand side. He was now fully "encapsulated" with Stan standing immediately behind him, and with a hand now resting on the lavatory edge on each side of Jimmy.

Jimmy could feel Stan's body against his back side as well as his arms on each side of himself. Now totally confused as to just 'what and why,' he looked in the mirror to see that Stan was calmly looking down to the base of Jimmy's neck, and was somewhat positioned in a silent stance. One arm resting on the lavatory edge on each side of Jimmy, and now his face only within inches of Jimmy's shoulder and neck. Jimmy stopped shaving. He calmly stood there and all his mind could manage right then was the big question, "Just what in the hell is going on here!?" He could feel Stan's body lean up against his, and if his feeling was right, it did feel as if maybe Stan was supporting a hard-on and it was pushing up against his body.

Standing there, completely confused as to just what was happening, Jimmy continued to watch in the mirror, and looked to his side to see the reflection of Stan calmly standing there, looking as if he was about to kiss his neck or shoulder. All of a sudden, but very calmly, Jimmy could tell that Stan had reached down and had loosened the towel around his waist and allowed it to fall to the floor. Now there was no question if Stan did or did not have a hard-on. He did! And Jimmy could feel it moving up against his bare buttocks, and he could also feel Stan stooping down some, so that the tip of it would find its direction in-between his butt cheeks.

Jimmy stood there with his hands firmly placed on the edge of the lavatory, and his mind swirling in circles wondering just what was happening. Confused, shocked, bewildered and stunned, he simply stood there and all of a sudden, realized that his traveling companion was actually in just about the right position to ram his ass full of cock, with one very firm feeling cock! He did not move! He froze in place! He wanted to yell questions of, "Just what in the hell is happening here," and "Stan what in the hell are you doing?" Wanting to and actually getting the words out were two very different things. The mind was working, and the mouth was not. Never had he ever had some other man get so close as to even seeing his bare ass, and now, with a man he had been friends with for at least five years, he was now standing there and feeling that man's cock pushing up against the inside of his butt cheeks, and actually feeling like it was getting closer and closer to his asshole. He knew he had Stan's cock right at his asshole, and it was obviously just about ready to get pushed in!

As Jimmy stood there in complete shock and confusion, he saw Stan grab the hand cream, squeeze some onto his hand, and then actually step back far enough to smear it on his rod. He then moved back into place, and slid his hand across Jimmy's chest to rub off the excess hand cream that was left on his hand.

Stunned, shocked and frozen into place, Jimmy realized that Stan had, in-fact, lubed up his dick and there could be only one reason that he would have done that, and that reason was only inches from the tip of his cock! "He's gonna fuck my ass, oh my gawd he's gonna fuck me," was really the only thing that Jimmy could process across his mind! "Oh, my God – oh my God – what do I do!? What do I do!?"

Wanting to move – or not wanting to move – not wanting to get fucked – but yet realizing that maybe, for some unexplained funny reason he should just let Stan do it, Jimmy was totally confused and just stood there in complete shock and somewhat fear. If he did let Stan poke him in the ass, what was that gonna be like? Was that gonna hurt? He had heard of guys getting a cock stuck up in his ass, and now he knew that this man, that was leaning up against him, was getting ready to do it to him, even though they had never even gotten close to discussing anything like this! They had been friends for about five years, and pretty close friends for at least two years and they had never talked about anything like this! They were each married men. The each had children! Their wives knew each other! They had traveled to other functions together before, and they had roomed together before, and never – never, had they even talked about sex, much more than maybe complaining about how one or the other one of them wished he could get it a little more often than he was. The normal man to man talk! The normal locker room or shower room type of talk that guys always do. But never, never anything like this! Never had either one of them ever approached the subject of gay sex! And this was not talk – this was action! Sheer bare skin-to-skin action, and Jimmy did not know how to handle it! He knew he was just about to get fucked in the ass, and he really did not know if that was gonna be okay, or if he needed to stop everything – right on the spot! He didn't want to offend Stan and he sure didn't want to lose a good friendship, and he sure didn't want to have to explain later to his wife why the friendship stopped, but did he really want Stan ramming his cock up in his ass!?

Jimmy stood there, leaning forward onto the lavatory, feeling Stan's dick moving its way up between his ass cheeks, and feeling Stan's torso leaning more and more onto his back. Stan's arms slowly moved closer and closer to Jimmy's sides and he managed to softly hug Jimmy in a very soft and gentle manner. Slowly Stan's left hand once again moved up and rested onto Jimmy's chest. Then the right hand did the same. Jimmy was now, fully enclosed with Stan's body on his back, his dick sliding up into his ass, and his arms hugging his body as his hands slid up and down the soft skin, but yet firm chest muscles and stomach muscles that Jimmy had!

Stunned, as if a marble statue, Jimmy just stood there and continued to look at himself and Stan in the mirror. He said nothing! He did nothing! The only thing that he could do, and he knew that was not working so well either, was to simply try and figure out just what in the hell was happening! Why was Stan, all of a sudden, this completely different person?

Stan's hands moved over to Jimmy's left tit, and to his right tit. Softly and very gently he moved his fingers together and allowed them to slightly pinch Jimmy's tits. Looking up and into the mirror, he watched as Jimmy looked back, but made no move. No good move, no smile, and yet no bad move, no frown! Stan smiled. Jimmy saw it. He still made no move. He simply looked directly into Stan's eyes, through the mirror.

Stan's hands moved gently across Jimmy's chest, and once again slightly touched and then slightly squeezed Jimmy's nipples. Surprisingly he heard Jimmy let out an inadvertent sigh. It was not expected, but it was not bad either. It was simply a release of air out of one very stressed body.

But yet, it was a good sign. It could have been a bad release, and it was not.

After some very gentle and some very exciting touching of Jimmy's chest and tits, Stan lowered his hands down, and with each hand grabbed the bottom of Jimmy's butt cheeks. Slowly, and as he watched Jimmy's expression in the mirror, Stan separated the cheeks, and slightly slid his rod up and into a more secured position. Jimmy did not flinch. He simply kept an eye in the mirror and watched Stan's facial actions. He did not say, "Go for it," nor did he say, "Stop it!" Silently he was allowing Stan to do as he wanted, and yet, still did not know why this was even happening, and he was still in a total state of confusion – still not knowing if what was happening, and what was about to happen, was good or not. Yes, he had heard of guys getting a dick up in their asses before, but he sure as hell never thought he'd be one of 'em. All he could even think about was stuff like, "I always figured if one guy wants to fuck another guy, he'd ask him first," and also things like, "do friends, all of a sudden, do this to a friend without even talking about it," "how in the hell can he even think that I'd let him put his cock up in my ass," and of course, "has he fucked some other guys sometime?"

Jimmy stood there, still leaning on the edge of the lavatory, totally silent, not saying anything, still feeling completely confused, and Stan continued to move his torso up closer and closer to his cock's planned destination, the sweet rose bud asshole. Without looking back to look at it, or even reaching back to feel it, Jimmy could tell that Stan's cock was definitely, definitely, very stiff and was standing almost straight up in the air, since it was pushing up on the bottom of his ass. It did almost feel as if maybe he was about to sit on the top of a fence post. He remembered how far Stan had stooped down, when this all got started, just to get the tip of his cock under his ass, so Jimmy knew it had to be more than just a short little cock.

As Stan moved closer and closer, Jimmy said nothing, still stunned about what was happening all of a sudden. This whole thing was so totally unexpected he really did not know exactly just what he should be doing or saying! He knew what was happening, or what was going to be happening. He could definitely feel the tip of that stiff cock poking and wanting to find the entry spot! Yet he still said nothing. Stan took that as an unspoken 'okay' to keep it up. With his left hand, he grabbed his dick, he aimed it, and the tip of his cock felt the edges of Jimmy's asshole! He listened to Jimmy and heard nothing negative, just some now rather deeper breathing, but nothing that was indicating that he was 'off base.' He silently grinned as he looked at his buddy in the mirror, and saw him looking back with no words of any threat.

Slowly Stan continued to move his torso forward, and softly he found his aim. Just as the tip of his cock touched 'the hole,' Jimmy slightly jerked.

Stan leaned down toward Jimmy's neck and softly asked, "You okay? You okay?" That was truly the very first thing said or spoken, since this entire episode was started, right after Stan just explained that he just wanted to get something off of the shelf!

Still stunned, and answering as he truly was, Jimmy attempted an, 'I guess. I guess. Stan, what in the hell are we doing man!? What in the hell are we doing?"

"Making ya feel better man – just making ya feel better! Just stand there and let me make you feel good. Okay? Okay?"

"Gawd man – I guess man – but Stan – I know what's going on here man, you're starting to fuck me, man, I know what's happening man, and I ain't never been fucked before! Stan, I've never done this! Stan, I've never done anything like this before, never! I've never played with a guy like this before! I've never had anything ever put up in my ass man, never."

"Yeah, I know man, I know! Something new and good for ya man, something new and good. Lean on that lavatory and just let me take care of stuff back here, okay? I'll be real gentle and nice to you, and you're gonna love it man, you're gonna love it!"

Now trying to trust his friend, and also trying to just go with the flow, Jimmy stood there and hung his head, feeling Stan's rod move up and in, farther and farther! A couple of times he jerked and attempted to readjust his body as he felt his backside getting fuller and fuller! He knew he sure was doing something new, but he was still wondering about the 'good' part of it. Once Stan had gotten the head of his cock up and in, and Jimmy did realize he had done that very carefully, his ass didn't hurt any, and he realized that Stan had actually managed to get it shoved up and in, without hardly any pain at all. Once that was managed, Jimmy did start to try and understand what Stan was saying about feeling good. He knew he had all of Stan's dick up in him, since he could feel Stan's crotch up against his ass. If he had been asked, yes, he would have had to admit it was feeling kinda good stuck up in there, but he was not ready to volunteer that information yet. He knew he was feeling a very different kind of a feeling back in his ass than he had ever experienced before, and being is such a state of confusion, as he knew he was right then, he really did not know if to admit, to even himself, that his ass was really feeling kinda good. He really did not know if he should expect anything to feel good back there or not! He knew he was now actually getting fucked in the ass, but he sure wasn't ready to tell anybody that maybe it actually felt good. In his mind, this wasn't over just yet, and he still did not know what was still gonna happen, nor how he was gonna feel until it was over! All he knew right then was that Stan had managed to stick his cock up in his ass, and everything so far was so good, but the fear of some kind of pain still stood. And besides, he was a man, with a man's dick now stuck up in his ass! This just was not right! He knew men were not supposed to have sex with another man! Never, had he ever had somebody doing anything like this to him before! He knew he had Stan's dick up and in him, and he knew that whenever

Stan pulled it back out, it had to come back out without any pain. His ass going shut really couldn't hurt. Actually he had to admit to himself that getting it stuck up in there really didn't hurt any either, well not much, so taking it back out sure shouldn't hurt any either! When it came out – but just not yet! He was realizing that he just didn't want Stan to pull it out yet. Not yet! No, not yet! He realized he wanted it left up in there for some more time. He liked the way it felt! He wanted to feel it up in there some more! He liked the idea that Stan was, in fact, up in his ass. This was totally something new, something totally unexpected!

For a few short moments, he had actually felt as if he had left his body and his head, and for a moment he did have the same childish feelings as the day, when he was only about twelve or thirteen and he found a sex magazine that his neighbor was throwing away, and as he looked at it, he kept looking around to make sure nobody saw him looking at it. Suddenly he felt as if he was twelve or thirteen again and once again sneaking in something very nasty and very dirty! Something that he was not supposed to be doing or looking at! After his short "out of body thoughts," suddenly he realized that he was now standing there, in the hotel room bathroom, completely bare assed, not even a towel around his waist, leaning on the lavatory, and all of a sudden, without any planning, he had a man's cock stuck all of the way up in his ass! He was standing there, looking in the mirror, eye to eye, at the man that had grabbed ahold of each side of his ass, pulled it open and then had slid all of his dick up, and in his ass, and he was not yelling at him to get it out! Never in a million years did he ever expect to be in a bathroom with some guy, especially when they were completely naked, let alone having that man grab and feel his ass and then stick his cock up in his ass. All of a sudden he felt as if maybe he was out in some dark, back, trashy alley doing something that he had always been told not to do! It excited him! All of a sudden he realized he was doing some of the same stuff that kids, much younger than he, did all of the time. Things he had read about, or heard about, but had never talked to anybody about. Things his mommy and daddy had told him never to do! Now, he was getting ass fucked, and he still had not, even yet, talked to anybody about doing it. It was just happening, and all of a sudden – he was glad! All of a sudden nothing seemed bad about it! All of a sudden his ass felt good, very full, but very good! He was still fully confused as to just why this was happening, but he was now starting to feel kind of on the 'glad side' that it was. The idea that Stan would ever do this, even if they had talked about it first, was way out of reach of being 'something that would ever happen,' but here he was, leaning on a lavatory edge, feeling Stan leaning up against his back, feeling Stan's arms around him and actually feeling quite excited that his ass was full of Stan's cock! He truly felt as if he was twelve or thirteen again, and really was out in the dark dirty back alley doing something dirty and nasty with somebody that he knew he was not supposed to be doing! He liked the feeling, the nasty, dirty feeling! He felt like he was a kid getting some sex for his very first time! All of a sudden, he actually had the feelings that maybe he was out on the street having sex and people were watching! He was feeling nasty and kinky, and he liked it!

He dropped his head, he closed his eyes, he grabbed onto the lavatory tighter, he bent his knees slightly, and as he let out a slight, "Yeah, man, yeah," he pushed his ass out! He was giving Stan his ass, and he was giving it to him without reservation or caution! His body actions actually screamed, "Take me, man, take me! Fuck it man, fuck it! You wanted it man, take it! Fuck my ass man, fuck me and fuck me good!!"

Suddenly Jimmy had become the aggressor and the man that needed to be satisfied!

Without knowing why in the hell this was now happening, Stan did not object, and he knew without question that Jimmy was – for some unexplained reason, was now really into what was going on, and he was now really going for it! Stan made sure that Jimmy was now truly getting fucked! Not just fucked, but fucked good and hard and good and rough! He could feel, even maybe coming up through his dick, that Jimmy was really enjoying this and was begging and begging for more and more if it! Jimmy's actions were yelling for, "More man, more! Harder man, harder! Rougher man, rougher!"

"Oh, man! Oh, shit, man! Oh, Stan do it, do it! Oh, Stan why in the hell didn't you fuck me years ago? Oh, Stan, fuck me, man, fuck me! Yeah, do it, do it! I knew two of my football buddies did this to each other back then, but I sure as hell never knew why! Now I do! Fuck me hard man, fuck me hard! Oh, God Stan – do it – do it man – do it! Ram it man! Ram it! Oh, Stan, do me then I gotta do you! Can I do you too!? Oh, Stan, thank God I needed to be cheered up man, thank God!"

Stan went to work on his man, and as he humped and pumped that tight muscled ass, he slid his hands down along the sides of Jimmy's body, then reached around to the front and with his left hand, grabbed the bag of nuts and slightly squeezed them so that Jimmy did know he had ahold of them, as he too grabbed ahold of one of the nicest, warmest, blood filled hard-ons, that he had felt, in a long, long time.

"Hey, Jimmy my man! You've got one hell of a hot dick here man, one hot dick! Hell yes you can fuck me, man, hell yes! I need that thing, I need it! It's been way too long since I've had a dick that big up in my chute – hell yes you can fuck me!"

Now looking into the mirror and into Stan's face with a completely new expression, Jimmy asked, "A long time!? Stan – how long? I guess my ass is not the first ass you've used then, right? You've fucked other guys, right? When I fuck you, I kinda guess it's not gonna be your first time getting fucked – is it?"

And as Stan pounded and pounded on Jimmy's ass, jerking and pulling him back and forth, away from, and back up against the lavatory cabinet, again and again, he looked up into the mirror, looked Jimmy eye ball to eye ball, and just grinned! Just one, very wide, grin!

FROM ACROSS THE STREET

As Greg was just coming in toward the living room from the den area, he heard someone knocking on side door. As he approached the door, he recognized a co-worker of Steve's, but did not know his name.

As he opened the door, he immediately said, "Hi."

"Hi. I'm Matt, I work with Steve, from across the street. I thought he and I were gonna be doing some work today, and I've been over there waiting for him, but he's not there, and – hey – I was wondering if maybe I could use your bathroom? I've gotta – kinda gotta go – and of course I can't just do it out in the yard."

Opening the door so that Matt could come on in, Greg replied. "Yeah, Hi, Matt. I'm Greg. I knew who you were when I saw you, but I've never known your name before. Sure, come on in, guy. Head right down that way, the bathroom is on the right."

Not being a person that checks out other guys, since Greg was a very happily married, big strong beefy type of a man of 34 and a father of two, he did think it was rather unusual that he did notice the tight firm butt on Matt as he walked past. Matt, apparently about 24 or 25 was not overly dressed, wearing only a tight pair of "the old style basketball shorts," (the type before they became skirts), and a tight very nice chest hugging and form fitting tight tank top, with just the simple word "Yeah" printed on the chest of it. That, he thought was rather interesting, in such as, "Yeah" to what?

As Matt returned to the kitchen area from the bathroom, he was still tucking in his meat stick and continuing to move it into a more comfortable or appropriate place. Noticing Matt's hand action on his crotch definitely did, of course, make Greg take notice, and as part of that "take notice" he did notice that Matt must be carrying a very nice piece of meat. It was showing very predominately!

"Huh, Greg. Do you mind if maybe I hang out over here and watch for Steve from here? It's really boring to just sit over there and not have anybody to talk to. I saw your wife and the kids leave a little bit ago. You busy? Do you mind?"

Standing there, leaning back up against the kitchen cabinet, Greg replied, "No! Mean – yeah – you can hang out here. We can see Steve's driveway from this window, and when he gets here, we'll see him. Hey, want something to drink? You're over 21 right? I've got some Bud, or if you want I got some Coke and some Sprite too."

"Hey, great man, I'd like the Bud. Yeah, I'm over 21. I'm 23 from about three months ago. Thought getting to 21 was never gonna happen though."

As Greg handed him the beer, he noticed Matt's eyes move ever so slightly down toward his crotch before he looked up and emphatically said, "Thanks man, thanks!" Then he sat on one of the kitchen chairs and asked, "Hey, Steve tells me you're a coach someplace right? That right?"

As Greg leaned against the kitchen cabinet, he looked at Matt and informed him that Steve was right – he was a coach at a Jr. High School in one of the suburbs across town. As he spoke, his eyes were constantly drawn to Matt's crotch, since it appeared that Matt just could not get that dick of his in the position of exactly where he wanted it. As he drank a couple of slugs from his beer, he also moved his dick more than once.

Coach Greg took a slug or two and continued to watch the action being so plainly being presented, rather full screen before him.

Putting together the very tight shorts, the question of the "Yeah" on his shirt, the firm tits that he now noticed sticking out from the chest in the tank top, and now – low and behold – now the tip of Matt's dick sticking out the bottom of his shorts, really did make Greg start wondering just exactly who was he talking to in his kitchen. And as he took another slug of the Bud, Greg took a good firm look and confirmed that the tip of that dick sticking out – was sticking out because the whole dick was hard! He was starting to get rather interested in just how much of a meat stick this guy was carrying with him. From that perspective, it looked like it could actually be bigger – longer and thicker, than his own, and he had always been rather proud of the extra big, ten and a half inch long black thick dick. As he looked at Matt, at Matt's crotch, at Matt's nice muscled chest, and of course at the two inches of bare dick that was now sticking out from the cover of his shorts, for the very first time while looking at a man, Greg realized that he was, himself, starting to get somewhat firm down there in the crotch area.

The conversation continued in a very casual way, discussions about the type of work Steve and Matt did together, how long each of them had lived in this particular area, and finally, with no surprise to Greg, the conversation finally got around to Matt and his girl friends, and then of course, finally to the, "I ain't getting any from any of my girls, and I'm about as horny as a guy can get!"

Suddenly, Matt blazingly pulled his dick out from under his shorts and pushed the bottom of his shorts up, stood up, moved over toward Greg, looked down at Greg's crotch, licked his lips quickly, jerked his own, now protruding, hard dick a couple of times and then asked, "Greg, can I feel your dick? Please, man, I wanna see how much dick you got! May I please, please? Please, can I feel it? You're such a really, really big black man and I really do wanna feel it and grab it, please! Please! I've never gotten to feel a big dick like this one on a black man before! Please, please!"

Stunned, confused, bewildered, and at the same time, getting somewhat turned on, Greg did not answer. He simply stood there and watched Matt move his hand out toward his crotch. As he watched the hand come toward himself, he felt his rod move and press up against the fabric of his own shorts. He looked down and saw what looked like a circus tent standing out in front. Mentally he said, "Oh, shit, man, oh shit! I've got a fucking hard-on man, I've got a hard-on! This guy has made me get a hard on! Crap man, I've gotten a hard-on cause of this guy!"

"Oh, man, oh man!" Matt almost screamed as he reached out and felt the major bulge sticking out of Greg's shorts. "Oh, Greg, oh Greg – I gotta see this thing man, I gotta see it!"

As Greg stood there still stunned, confused, and bewildered, he did not say anything nor move any as he looked down, watched Matt pick up the tail of his t-shirt, slide his fingers into the top of Greg's shorts, then slowly and softly pull them out and then down to let Greg's dark mahogany, thick, cut dick, pop out and point directly at himself. "Oh, shit Greg, oh shit! Oh, Greg, this is pretty man, this is pretty! I've never done anything with a black man's dick before, but man, I'm wishing like hell now that I had been, and a long time ago! If they're all like yours man, I wish I had been sucking on black guys years ago! Oh, your dick is pretty man, it is pretty! It looks like black leather man, just like black leather!"

"Hey, Matt, Matt! Matt, we shouldn't be doing this stuff man, we shouldn't be! Come on, let me put it away man, let me put it away!"

"Oh, Greg, please! Please! Man, I gotta play with that thing man, I gotta. How long's your wife and the kids gonna be gone? How long till they come back?"

"Matt, I don't know, I really don't! That's why we gotta stop this stuff right now! They could come home at any minute man – any minute. We gotta stop this!"

"Come on. Come on! Let's go over to Steve's and use his place. I saw you looking at my dick – I know you were looking at it! Please, please!"

"Go over to Steve's place? What do you mean – go over to Steve's place?"

"I've got a key to his house! I've known all along they weren't gonna be here today. They went up to the state park fishing this weekend. I knew they weren't gonna be here! Greg, I said I was waiting on him, just so I could try and do something like this with you. I've wanted to see you naked ever since the very first time I saw you about four or five months ago. I've watched you a lot since then, man! Whenever I could, whenever I was over at Steve's place. He and I weren't gonna do any work today! I did this to see if I could maybe have some time with you like this!"

"You're kidding, right? You're kidding?"

Standing there, with Greg's big sausage hard-on meat firmly placed in his hand and rubbing it back and forth as he did, Matt replied, "No. No! I'm not kidding. Please, man, please! I gotta suck on this big thing! I gotta man, I gotta! I gotta see how much of it I can take man, I gotta. Man I am so fucking hot for you and this dick right now man, I am! I'm fucking hot as hell!"

"You've got a key to Steve and Jeannie's house? Is that right?"

"Yeah, man, yeah. They wanted me to have it so that in case I had to come by the house to get something for Steve, and Jeannie wasn't here, I could get into his workshop! Please, Greg! Please!! I really wanna play with this thing! I gotta do it man, I gotta! This thing is gorgeous man, fucking gorgeous! You ever play with guys? You play with guys? Please, please, I gotta have you play with me!"

"No Matt, no! No I don't play with guys! And besides, until today I've never even gotten a hard-on, just by looking at some guy! Yeah, I gotta admit I did today, but then you had your dick out the bottom of your shorts and you were playing with it, and guys just don't normally do that in front of other people. Yeah, man, yeah, gotta admit, that kinda made me feeling kinda horny, man, kinda. I mean after all, Matt, you are one hot built looking guy. And – I got a question. Just how often do you wear those shorts? I swear if you bend over in 'em, they are gonna rip out completely in the ass. How often you wear them?"

"I don't. I mean, not anymore I don't! I did today, cause I wanted to look really hot and sexy to see if I could get something like this started, and I think it worked. It did, didn't it? Did it work?"

Still leaning back on the kitchen cabinet, now looking down at not only his own crotch, but at Matt's also, Greg reached out, took ahold of Matt's dick and said, "I guess! Yeah, I guess man, I guess! But Matt – I've never done sex with a guy before! You understand that? I've never done anything with another guy before! You understand?"

"Yeah, man, yeah! I understand, I understand! Oh, Greg, this means you're gonna go do it with me, are ya? Oh, please tell me you are, please tell me you are!"

"Yeah, yeah I guess. I've never done anything with some guy before, but I've often wondered what doing something like that would be like, so yeah, but we gotta get out of here right now or my wife and the kids are gonna be back and then it's not gonna work."

Now that Matt had been successful in his little attempt at getting Greg to agree to some action together, and now that Greg had admitted to himself that if he was ever going to do something as stupid as have sex with some guy, this Matt guy was a pretty good piece of meat to do it with.

They quickly headed for Steve's house, agreeing that if Greg's family did happen home while he was across the street, their story would be they were working on Steve's house for him, while he was gone.

Hurrying up the drive toward the house, Matt stopped at his truck and grabbed what looked like a shaving kit and two folded towels out of the passenger side window. Just as quickly as they entered the house through the back door, which was the door that Matt had a key for, he said, "Hey, man, let's go use the living room. We can lay on the floor. I don't wanna mess up a bedroom or nothing. Okay?"

Responding with a "Yeah," Greg and Matt headed in there as Greg asked. "Hey, Matt, you're sure they're out of town today? You real sure they're gone and they ain't gonna be coming home? You sure?"

"Yeah, man, yeah! I'm sure! I helped Steve get his stuff ready to go yesterday! I helped him with his tackle box and his poles. They're camping out on Baylee Ridge, and I helped 'em get their camping stuff together. They're gone man, they're gone!"

"Huh, Matt!? Matt, does Steve know you play with guys? He know what you do?"

"No! No he don't. I keep telling him about my girls and all the pussy I get, but I never tell him about all the guys and all the ass and all the dick I get, too!

"Come here man, let me get you all stripped down and naked, and then let me finally see you all bare and naked! Oh, yeah, man, oh yeah! I've wanted to see all of you like this ever since I saw you that first time bending over and taking something out of the trunk of your car! You got one hell of a hot ass on you, man, one hell of a hot ass! The first time I saw it, I wanted to come over there and push my face right up in there! I did!"

As the two men stood in the middle of the living room and continued to strip each other fully bare, Greg replied, "Well let me tell you something, little stud muffin. You're hanging one hell of a hot dick on yourself, and especially for some young white guy, and you got one hell of a hot body too! You in gymnastics or something? You got one hell of a hot body on you!"

"No, not gymnastics, but I do a lot of weight room working out! I used to be real skinny and I'm trying to put on a lot of bulk and tying took a lot more like you! I wanna be big and beefy and hunky just like you! I guess that's why I got all horny for you the very first time I saw you! Greg, I've jerked off a lot of nights just wishing you were in bed with me! That's why I did the funny thing I did today! I had to see if I could do it with you, and I figured today was my chance if I was gonna have one. You are fucking hot man, fucking hot! Your body is so pretty! It is! Oh, man look at that cock and you've got the nicest round butt! You're all man – you are! Big, strong, muscled and hung like a horse! Greg, I knew that whenever I got a chance to see that thing it was gonna be one of the biggest sticks that I've ever seen, or probably will ever see! Oh, it is so pretty, it is! I know you're not supposed to call some part of a man 'pretty,' but seriously, that is what that thing is! Come here, man, I gotta taste your dick and I gotta taste your ass! Give me your dick and then I wanna eat your ass!"

With Greg standing in the middle of the living room, and Matt now down on his knees in front of him, and with all ten and a half inches of Greg's enormous big black pole stuck firmly down in his throat, Matt was pulling Greg's body up closer and closer so that he could take more dick, as if there were more to be taken. For a good ten minutes or more, Matt sucked on Greg's cock, sucked his nuts into his mouth and rolled 'em around and around in his mouth, licked and kissed his crotch, and used each and every inch of Greg's most private places, and attempted to suck all of the fluids out of his body, right through his dick. He spread Greg's legs apart, and managed to actually get his face up and under his ass, and lick on his asshole! He had told Greg he wanted to eat his ass, and that was exactly what he was doing! He grabbed onto Greg's legs and forced his face up and into his ass as far as he could!

Matt told Greg to bend over some so he could get his face up in there tighter and really get to his velvet lined asshole. Pulling Greg back as much as possible, and pushing his face up and in as much as possible, Matt ate Greg's ass out, totally and completely!

Suddenly Matt pulled off, reached over and grabbed one of the towels he had brought in from the truck, laid it on the floor, grabbed the shaving kit, took out some lube, rubbed it on Greg's dick, and without even asking, he told Greg to, "Fuck me hard and rough, man – hard and rough! I want you to really know what fucking some guy's ass can really feel like! Fuck me and do it hard! Fuck me rough!"

Laying himself down on the towel and offering his ass hole to Greg by reaching back and pulling his butt cheeks apart, as if to let Greg know where the hole was at, Matt again said, "Fuck me hard and rough man – hard and rough! Give me that dick man, give me that dick!"

As if he had done this many times with other guys and their assholes, Greg aimed it, rocked back and forth on it a few times, and then drove it home! Immediately he took all of Matt's ass, and Matt's ass took all of his big, thick, stiff, cock!

As his rod hit the bottom of the chute, Greg let out with an, "Oh, yeah, man, oh yeah! Oh, Matt this feels so fucking good, man, this is good! Oh, Matt, your hard ass is great! Oh, shit, man, I never thought going up in some guy's ass could feel anything like this! Oh, Matt, this is fucking great, man, this is great! You okay, man, you okay?"

"Oh, yeah, man, oh yeah! Greg, I am more than okay! Greg, I know I've never had that much dick slammed up inside of me before! It is fucking big, but it is feels fucking great! I feel like you just ran something like an ice cream truck up in my ass man, I do! Fuck me, man, fuck me! Fuck me hard, do me hard!"

Suddenly Matt and Greg heard someone yelling, "What in the hell is going on in here, and who in the hell are you guys!!? Who are you!!??"

Somebody had come into the house, and in their excitement and with the groaning and moaning going on during the rough, fucking session, neither man heard the back door open!

"Who in the hell are you guys?"

Looking up at the surprise visitor, Matt did not answer but rather asked his own question. "Who in the hell are you!? Who are you?"

"I'm Jason, Steve's brother! Who in the hell are you?"

"I'm Matt, I work with Steve – kinda for Steve."

"Oh, so you're the one they couldn't get in touch with today then, right?"

"I don't know – did they try to call me?"

"Yeah, they did! Jeannie wasn't sure if she turned off the back sprinkler and they wanted you to come over and check on it, but then Steve finally called me and asked me to check. He sure as hell never told me I'd be coming in here and finding some good hot sex stuff going on though! Who's the big guy fucking you? Who's he?"

After the first few rather tense minutes of the surprise visit, everybody got pretty well calmed down, and Matt managed to explain "why" they were there. Jason actually ended up finding it rather funny and interesting, to say the least!

"Jason, please, please don't tell Steve or Jeannie that we did this here! Please, man, please!" Matt pleaded and begged. "I didn't think anything like this would happen if we came over here for a few minutes! Please, Jason, please!"

Matt and Greg were still lying on the floor, so Jason looked down and said, "Tell you what, man – tell you what! I could pretty well get your ass in one hell of a lot of trouble with what I found going on in here today, but turn around is kinda fair play, don't you think?

"Looking up at Jason, and still very concerned and very nervous about what Jason could do to both him and Greg, Matt said, "Yeah, yeah, I guess so. Jason, I don't know what you're saying to me, what are you telling me?"

"Matt, my man, your ass is in one hell of a lot of trouble! Agreed?"

"Yeah, I know, I know! Please, Jason, please, don't tell Steve! Please!"

"Okay man. I do something for you – you do something for me – okay?

"Yeah, yeah! What? What do you want me to do?"

"I want you to get up off of the floor, let me lay there on that towel, then you let your muscled hunk of a buddy there pound my ass like he was pounding yours, and then I want you squatted in front of my face so I can eat your dick. I want your dick in my mouth while I swallow that big black one up in my ass! It's been probably about four or five years since I've had a chance to do something good and wild like this with two hot and hunky guys, so all I can say is, if you don't want me telling Steve anything about what was going on in here, then you two better use me and use me good! Fuck my face and fuck my ass! Fuck me and let me eat that big white ice cream cone you got there, man! I heard you telling your big man here that you thought he had driven an ice cream truck up in your butt when he fucked it, so I'm gonna let him drive that truck up in my ass, and then I'm gonna eat that ice cream cone you've got hanging out there!" And with a big grin on his face, he added, "Do it or I'm gonna tell, understand?"

With one big sigh of relief, Matt yelled out, "Hell yes, I understand, hell yes! Oh, man, thanks man, thanks! Greg, fuck him in the ass! I'm gonna fuck him in the mouth! Oh, man, this is great, this is great!"

As Jason laid down on the floor, he looked at Greg and made one request. "Hey, man, it's been years and years since I've had a cock stuck up in there! My wife just ain't got the tool to do it! And of the dicks I've had up in me, not one of 'em was ever as fucking big as that telephone pole of a rod you got on you, so go slow on me, man – go slow! I want it and I want all of it deep – all the way in but just take it slow going in! Take it slow and easy cause I'm gonna have Matt's dick in my mouth, and if you make my ole butt hole hurt, I'm gonna bite the hell out of his dick, so unless you wanna hear him screaming like hell, go easy back there, real easy!"

As Greg mounted Jason's ass, he then asked, "So man! I kinda guess maybe from what you've been saying here, you played with some guys before."

Turning his head so he could answer Greg, Jason replied, "Yeah, used to. Used to, but it's been some time now. Why? Why'd you wanna know?"

"Well our man Matt there has got a pretty good swinger for a white guy, but this thing, that is just about to go up in your ass, has never been stuffed down in some guy's throat before, so I just thought that I'd let you know that after you get done sucking on Matt's meat, and eating his ice cream cone as you called it, I'd let you try some good old chocolate ice cream fudge bar and see how it tastes! So when I get done ramming this pole up in your butt hole, I want you to suck it dry for me and let me see what a good strong mouth feels like sucking on it! Okay? Deal?"

"Oh, shit, man! Are you kidding? I've never sucked on a dick that big before! I don't think I can do that, I don't! It's too fucking big! I've never sucked on guys much before, and honestly man, that thing is really a hell of a lot bigger than I think I can get in my mouth or in my throat! Please, don't make me do that! Matt's here is big enough for me, seriously man – seriously!"

Matt looked at Greg and begged, "Greg, me – please – me! Greg I wanna suck on it – please! Please, let me do it! I wanna do it! I wanna see if I can take it or not, I do! That's why I came over to your place today! I wanted to see it, and then see if I can take it and suck it off! Please, Greg, please let me do it!"

Looking back at Matt, Greg replied, "Deal man, deal! Guess maybe you're the bigger man here today then aren't you? Yeah, just as soon as I get done giving ole Jason a kid or two, then you are gonna do it! I honestly thought maybe you'd be saying it was too big, but hey, if you want it – you've got it! We'll let Jason here eat some ass out while you take my dick, okay? That okay with you Jason?"

"Yeah, man, yeah! Yeah, I'll eat ass! I'll eat ass, chew on some nuts, and maybe do Matt's ole rod again, but honestly man, that big long thing you got there, that's just too much for this guy! I'd never get that in my mouth, so I just ain't even gonna try! It's pretty – it's pretty, but it's just too fucking big! In my ass, it's great! Great – fuck me, man, fuck me and give me those two kids you mentioned a minute ago. Yeah, yeah – I wanna feel you giving me those kids! Fuck me, fuck me hard!"

And with that, Greg did Jason like he'd never been done before, and also made him just a little sorry he had probably turned down the greatest, biggest, stiffest, strongest, and thickest offer and opportunity ever offered to him.

As he laid there and fully felt every slam and bang going into his ass, Jason pondered over and over just how he could tell Greg that he was wrong, and yes, he did want to eat that dick, or at least as much of it as he could! He decided lying there and getting the hell pounded out of his ass, that yes – he did have to do it – yes he did have to eat that dick! He decided that he simply could not turn down this great of an offer. If he could do Matt – then he could do Greg – or at least choke trying! He knew he'd be able to get together again with Matt sometime, since he worked with Steve – but would he ever get a chance to do this with big Greg, again? He knew he had to do it now and not lose the chance at hand! It just might never happen again! Laying there, getting pounded like a beef steak getting tenderized, he decided that before this day was over – yes, he wanted that rod in his back-end, and also as far down his throat as he could go! He knew he wanted to do anything and everything he could, just like Matt did! All of a sudden, 'the bigger – the better!'

LET'S JUST GO SKINNY DIPPING!

"Hey, Jim, come on, let's go hit the pool!"

"Hit the pool!? You mean, go swimming?"

"Yeah, yeah! Today's the warmest day we've had yet, and I think going for a swim would feel good! Come on – wanna?"

"Bill, I didn't bring any trunks! I didn't know we were gonna go swimming – I didn't bring any trunks!"

"Hey, Jim, who cares? It's just you and me and the gals and the kids are gonna be gone till probably five or later, so let's just go skinny dipping! I've seen your bare ass before and you've seen mine before, so what's the big deal? Nobody can see into the backyard anyway! Come on!"

"Hey, if you want to, let's do it!"

Jim and Bill were old time friends that had grown up together through junior high and high school, and after going to college and each getting a degree, returned back to the 'old hometown' had married, had kids and continued their friendship.

Bill was thirty-four, was a construction manager for a large home building company. His legs looked like he climbed a ladder all day!

Jim was also thirty-four and was the district manager for a health club company. Obviously he used the health clubs to his physical advantage.

Each of the two had been very active in high school sports and fortunately due to their jobs had managed to maintain most of their hunky younger high school and college day builds! The active sports involvement and the active physical employments was definitely a strong element in the continuing friendship.

As they were headed out the door, towel in hand but bare asses well showing, Jim stopped, looked at Bill, and said, "The pizza! We ordered the pizza. Delivery guy's gonna be coming shortly."

"Oh, yeah! Yeah, forgot about that! Oh, hey, no big deal. It'll be Randy and hey, when I hear him drive up or ring the door bell, I'll just yell at him to bring it out back."

"Even though we're naked!?"

"Yeah, no problem. I was in the pool one day last year when he came by and I was swimming naked then too, so no big deal. He didn't mind any then, I guess. Anyway he never said anything about it. He just grinned and laughed! I'll just make sure it's Randy before I tell him to bring it out back. No big deal!"

Deciding that Bill knew best and what was okay, Jim threw his towel across the back of one of the patio chairs, opened a Bud from the cooler they had brought out, sat it on the edge of the pool, and did a deep-end dive into the pool.

Bill did similar and ended up close to Jim, kicking and splashing the cool pool water as he commented about how refreshing the water did feel.

"Hey, Randy! Randy, is that you!?"

"Yeah – yes it is! I've got the pizza!" The voice from the side yard yelled back, without seeing the person yelling to him.

"Randy, we're out back! Bring it out here. The side gate's open!"

With both of the swimmers now at the edge of the pool, resting with their arms up on the edge of the pool, they watched as Randy opened the side gate and came in with the ordered pizza.

"Hey, guy! Thanks!" Bill hollered as Randy sat the pizza box on the patio table. "Randy, there's fifteen bucks there stuck under that dish. Keep the extra for your tip!" Bill hollered and instructed.

"Thanks, man, thanks! Appreciate that! I really do! That water looks pretty good right now! Cool?"

"Yeah, it does feel good! This is the first time we've really used it any this year! Does feel good though! Jim didn't bring any trunks with him since we hadn't planned on swimming, so as you can well tell, we're kinda doing the ole skinny dipping thing. I didn't figure you'd mind if we were kinda in the raw when you got here. That's why I hollered to make sure it was you and not somebody else delivering the pizza."

"I guess that maybe your wives aren't here then, right?"

"Oh, yeah! They took the kids to some movie that they all wanted to see, so we're just doing the guy thing. Randy, meet Jim Brooker. Close friend of mine!"

Looking at Jim, Randy came closer to the edge of the pool, stooped down, extended his hand for a handshake, and said, "Hi! I'm Randy Wilson. Glad to meet you!"

The two men shook hands, and Randy stood back up, looked at Bill and asked. "Hey, Bill, I'm done for the day except for turning in the money, would you mind if I joined you guys for a few minutes?"

Bill replied, "No! If you want to – sure! Gotta strip down, though, since I don't have any trunks out here to give you. Gotta do the naked thing like us! Okay?"

As Randy, the hunky-built twenty-four year old pizza driver and part time bar tender replied, "Yeah, yeah," he grabbed the bottom of his pullover shirt, ripped it up and off his head, and then got his shoes and socks off. Both Jim and Bill interestingly watched as Randy's beautiful, furry and muscular chest came into full view. Neither man mentioned it, nor made any open comment about it, but they each did admire it. Bill did notice that Jim seemed to pay a little bit of extra attention!

Finally Randy unbuckled his slacks and to the shock of Jim and Bill, let 'em drop, showing no briefs, but instead one healthy, long, uncut, meaty, thick dick, with an even larger and thicker mushroom head. Neither man said anything, yet each man definitely noticed the manhood their pizza driver did have. Once again, Bill thought perhaps Jim had zeroed in on that rod and its flavorful sight!

As Randy walked to the deep-end of the pool, Jim and Bill looked at each other and grinned as if to say, "Gawd man, did you see that!?"

Bill and Jim were still standing against the edge of the pool, in the shallow end when Randy dove in.

As Randy dove in, Jim and Bill looked at each other again and shook their heads in amazement and disbelief. Suddenly both men jumped and attempted to turn.

"Whoa, whoa, what in the hell!? Jim let out rather quickly, at the same time as Bill yelled, "Hey, what in the hell!?"

Trying to turn and look down into the water, Jim realized that Randy had his face pushed up against his bare butt, his lips solidly placed on his ass, and at the same time, Bill realized that Randy had his hand up and under his crotch, and had a firm tight grip on his nuts!

"What in the hell?! What in the hell is happening here!?" Jim attempted to ask, of nobody in particular, since Randy was completely underwater and there was no way to ask him. Plus his face was completely buried in the crack of Jim's ass.

Bill was also trying to look in the water to figure out just what was happening, but as he attempted to move away from the pool edge, Randy pulled Bill closer to himself by hugging his leg against his chest and his hand held Bill's nuts even tighter! Bill was firmly trapped by Randy's hug – and did not attempt any escape.

Then, Randy popped up from down beneath the water level and took a deep breath.

Bill looked at him and asked with emphasis, "Randy, what in the hell is happening!? What are you doing!?"

As Randy re-grabbed Bill's cock, this time from the front side, he also reached over toward Jim and also grabbed ahold of his too.

"Oh, man, both of you guys are so hot! Bill, you have got one hell of a hot dick!" Then looking at Jim, he almost screamed, "Oh, man! You've got the ass of hell! Oh, man, I wanted to stay down there and suck on that ass, I did! Man I just wanted to suck it dry! God, you two are so fucking hot!"

Completely confused and bewildered, both Bill and Jim stood there and listened to what Randy was telling them. They appreciated what they were being told, yet were rather shocked. And they were each allowing their respective cocks to be pulled on as Randy slowly pulled and gripped them tighter and tighter. Neither man forced him to let loose!

Bill again asked, "Randy, what in the hell is happening!? What are you doing!?"

"Oh, Bill! Bill you guys are so fucking hot! Both of you guys are so fucking hot to me! Please, Bill, please Jim, don't be mad at me! When I dove in, I had to just come over here and get both of you guys! Oh, guys, both of you are so fucking hot to me!"

Still standing there, still bewildered and confused, Jim asked, "Randy, what you doing? What's going on here?"

Looking at Jim, Randy replied, "Oh, man, I gotta feel you! Please, let me lick on you! I gotta feel both of you guys! Please! Please, just let me slide my hands up and down on both of you guys, please!? Please?"

Not really knowing just what to do, both Jim and Bill simply stood there and watched as Randy stooped down beneath the water, keeping a hand on each man. He slid his hand up and down their torsos and around their backs and up between the cheeks of their asses then down along the side of their massive legs, then inside of a leg, then up against their crotches and finally grabbed ahold of each of the two bags. First he leaned over and licked the best he could on Jim's bag and dick then he turned to Bill and did the same. Finally, he had to come up for air, and as he did he continued to slide his hand up both of the hot torsos. Finally he let his hands rest on a nipple of each man! "Oh, gawd men, you are so fucking hot to me!"

Taking a big breath, Randy then added, "Oh, men, you are both so fucking hot! Men, I haven't done something like this for a long time." Then without saying anything further, he once again stooped down under the water, grabbed onto Bill's dick, opened his mouth and put his mouth on Bill's cock. He sucked, and to his pleasure, felt it getting stiff. For only a minute or less, he sucked on it, and he then had to come back up for air. As he did, he looked at Jim, and said, "Now you! Now you! I'm gonna suck on yours now!"

Randy sank down under the water, grabbed ahold of Jimmy's dick, placed his mouth up close to it, put his mouth on it, and sucked it all into his throat. Again he was smiling to know that this dick was also getting stiff. He pulled off, stood up, looked at first Bill, then Jim, and said, "Come on men, let's get up by the steps! Please, please! I gotta get your hot bods up there where I can suck on both of you out of the water! Please, please!"

Both Jim and Bill were feeling completely confused and frustrated about just what was happening, but neither man seemed to know exactly how to handle the situation. Neither man said anything.

With Randy having a hand on each man, he started to walk up the sloping pool bottom, up toward where he could get his two hot subjects up into shallower water where he could suck on them, and play with them and also have his face up out of the water.

Silently, as if not knowing what else to do, both Jim and Bill moved along. The three men approached the shallow end of the pool and Randy stooped down and once again took Bill's dick into his mouth. He had his left hand wrapped around Bill and had it firmly placed on Bill's right butt cheek. His right hand was wrapped around Jim's dick, and was slightly pulling it back and forth. He knew the dick in his mouth, and the dick in his hand, were each getting firmer and stiffer! He was sucking stronger and stronger, and he was also pulling harder and harder!

As they stood there in bewilderment, Bill finally looked over toward Jim and softly said, "God, this is different! Never had this done before."

Looking down at Randy and watching him stroke his dick back and forth and, once in awhile, grab onto a nut or two, Jim just simply uttered, "Yeah, yeah."

With both men leaning back against the side of the pool, Randy now had complete control over his two hot men of muscle, as he slowly continued to slide his hands up and down on the two hot bodies, and occasionally stand up just a little taller to take one of the four hot male tits into his mouth and suck on it. With each new movement or action, he carefully listened for any negative comment that could tell him that he was now moving in the wrong direction. He got none! He was one young man completely enjoying the taste and feel of two remarkably hot built men, ten years his senior. He was in heaven!

Both Bill and Jim were leaning back with their hands resting on the pool deck. That position actually made each man presenting his full frontal position, as if offering it fully and freely to Randy for all and any of his desires. And Randy was using each body – all of its muscles, its fuzzy hair, its individual exterior and its interior spots – to the extent that he could to his full and exciting use! His only trouble was in getting to each of the two hot bodies as fast as he wished he could. Each time he slid a finger up and under one man's bag, and had his other hand on the other man's tit, he wildly wished that he had two more hands to use, to grab another tit, another dick, another bag, another ass or even another asshole.

When he put his finger up into Bill's asshole, his finger slid in, and he felt Bill push forward, as if to plead for, "More – more!"

As his left hand was securely placed up and under Bill's crotch and his finger was invading Bill's tight ass, he then slid his right hand up and under Jim's crotch, and allowed his right index finger to invade that tight warm hole, too. He heard both men make a slight beautiful, beautiful, sound of, "Oh, oh! Oh, man, oh!"

Randy knew he was hitting the right spots, slightly tucked inside of the ass of each of his hot, hunky, muscular, playmate toys!

As Randy stood there, a finger, of each hand, up in the warm asshole of each of his hot and hunky men, he slowly leaned forward and slid his tongue up and down the muscular fronts of both of his men. Licking up and down and then sliding down even farther, he licked and sucked on each of the hot and now stiff dicks that were pointing directly toward his face.

"Oh, men! Oh, guys, you taste so fucking good! Oh, men, I'm loving this!" Randy exclaimed as he first sucked on one man, then the other, then back to the original and back and forth five or six times!

Suddenly and without any warning at all, Bill brought his right hand back around and took Randy's left tit into his hand. Then he said, "Hey, Jim, come on man, pinch his other tit! Let him know he's got a couple of guys here that are having some fun! Pinch him tight!"

"Oh, my gawd, man – oh my gawd! Oh, yeah, man – oh yeah! Oh, men! Oh, men, thanks!" Randy just almost screamed out, very loud. "Yes, yes, yes! Oh, men thanks, thanks! Oh, men do me, play with me men, play with me! Do me! Thanks men, oh thanks men!"

As Randy was very profoundly exclaiming his excitement, Bill brought his left hand out front, reached down and took ahold of Jim's hard, stiff rod.

Jim flipped his head sideways to look at his buddy, and just asked, "Bill? Bill?"

"I gotta man, I gotta! He's got me so fucking hot here, I gotta feel you! Come on man, grab me! Please, take my dick in your hand Jim! Come on! Jim, let me feel you grab my dick! Please! Please! Please!"

Being very cautious and moving very slowly, Jim did finally reach over and take Bill's dick into his hand. At first he just slightly held it, but then as Bill kept thrusting his body back and forth, as if he really did want Jim to take it stronger and to jerk it harder, all of sudden Jim acted as if he finally understood what Bill wanted him to do, and he reacted.

Watching both his own dick getting played with, and also looking over toward Jim to watch his own hand jerking and playing with Jim's cock, Bill then pinched Randy's tit even tighter.

"Oh, Randy, Randy, suck me off man, suck me off!" Bill suddenly demanded. "Suck me, I gotta cum man, I gotta cum!"

With Bill's sudden and unexpected demand, Randy immediately threw his mouth onto Bill's cock and sucked on it as hard as he possibly could!

"Yeah, man, yeah! Oh, yeah Randy, do it man, do it!" Bill was yelling for Randy to suck on him harder and harder, until almost without warning he firmly stated, "Oh, man, I gotta shoot man – I gotta shoot! Randy I'm gonna cum man, I'm gonna cum!!"

Jim could tell just when his buddy, Bill, finally shot off. He watched his body go stiff and rigid as his face tightened up and his entire being went rigid and solid. He watched Bill glaze off into space as he also watched his torso, his dick, his bag of nuts and everything else completely offer itself to Randy and his strong sucking mouth. Bill was in complete submission to his sucker! And Jim could tell! He knew what was happening!

"Oh, man, oh man! Oh, Randy, man that was good, that was so fucking good!" Then, looking over toward Jim, Bill said, "Hey, man, let him do you! Come on, let him suck you! You will not believe it man, you will not believe it!"

Looking over to Jim, but without saying anything, Randy asked with his eyes, "You want it? You want it?"

Looking back at Randy, standing there right there before him and his major hard on, Jim didn't answer with words either, but just with his eyes and expression. Randy knew he had another man who was wanting his dick taken care of. Immediately, he leaned down and took Jim's cock into his mouth. He sucked strongly!

Bill was slowly regaining his normal composure after his explosive cum shot, and he continued to reach over and slightly rub his buddy's arms and shoulders as he got his dick sucked on very strongly.

After about six or eight minutes of ragging, sucking and playing with all of his available body parts, Randy had now gotten Jim to the major exciting point of "no return," as if any man ever wanted to 'return,' when he reaches this point.

Jim let out with a very solid, "Oh, me – oh me! Oh, men, I'm gonnnnna – I'm gonnnnna! Randy – Randy, I'm gonna shoot, man! I'm gonnna shoot! Oh, yeah, oh yeah, oh yeah!"

All three men, and especially Jim, knew he was exploding inside, and that explosion was just about to come flying out of the tip of his dick. And it did! It did! Randy grabbed ahold of him and held him tight as he took all of the warm thick man juices, that Jim had just shot, down into his throat. As he swallowed as quickly as he could, he managed to massage both sides of Jim's body, up and down, and definitely included the upper insides of his stout and strong legs. Slowly he raised his hands up into Jim's crotch area as far as he could place 'em, and he then strongly massaged Jim's bag of nuts as he looked up and asked, "Okay? You okay, man? I liked that, I did! I did!"

Slowly Randy stood up, pushed both men together, shoulder to shoulder and gave them a bear hug. He hugged Bill up close and laid his face on his shoulder, and then did the same thing to Jim. Both men silently stood there and slightly hugged back. They were still in somewhat of a state of confusion, since it was openly obvious that neither one of them expected anything like this to happen!

All three men now stood there, and all three men had major erections showing.

Bill felt Randy's stiff rod pushed up against himself, and he looked down at it. Slowly, he dropped his hand and took it in his hand. Looking over at Jim, he slowly said, "Jim, look at the size of this fucking thing! Look how big it is!"

Jim looked down and watched Bill slide his hand back and forth on Randy's oversized rod. "Oh, shit, man, what a fucking dick! Randy, you got one hell of a big dick!" Jim expounded with a great degree of jealously in his voice.

Randy smiled as he looked down to watch Bill playing with his dick, and he then suggested, "Come on Jim, grab my balls for me, man, grab my balls. I want both of you hot looking men feeling me up at the same time!"

As Jim did reach down and cup his hand under Randy's bag of nuts, Randy softly said, "Oh, yeah, men, oh, yeah! Oh, thank you guys, thank you! I love that, I love that! Hey, guys, I gotta jerk it off! I gotta cum! Will you guys play with me and feel me and maybe pinch my tits some if I get up out of the pool, and jerk off over there by the flower bed? Will you guys kinda play with me some, please?"

Bill looked at Jim; Jim looked back at Bill and then said, "Yeah! Yeah, we will, man – we will. Randy, this is all new to both of us, but you sure did take care of both of us, so yeah, we'll do whatever you need us to do so you can jerk off and cum, too! Come on, guys, let's get out of the water and get ole Randy jerked off. Come on, guys."

All three men stepped up and out of the pool and headed over to toward the edge of the yard. Randy grabbed onto his dick and started jerking it back and forth. Bill stood to his left and had one hand back on Randy's butt and his other hand up on Randy's left tit. He squeezed both.

Jim was on Randy's right side and he too had a hand on Randy's butt, but his right hand was cupped up and under Randy's bag.

"Oh, men, yeah! Oh, yes, men – yes! Oh, guys, play with me please! Bill pinch that tit, pinch that tit! Oh, yes man, oh yes! Harder man – harder, harder! Please, harder, make me feel it! Yeah – do it – do it!"

Bill pinched Randy's tit just about as hard as he thought a man could take, but to his surprise he found out that Randy was able to take a hell of a lot more pain in his tits than he ever imagined that a man could handle. He pinched tight, very tight, not only his left tit, but on his right tit also!

"Jim, grab 'em man, grab 'em! Yeah, tighter man, tighter! Grab 'em man, gab those balls tight really tight! Make me squeal, man, make me squeal! Oh, men, oh men, I'm about to let it all fly! Oh, guys, yeah keep it up – keep it up! Yeah, pinch me, pinch me, pinch me tight! Grab my nuts, grab my nuts! Oh, yeah, oh yeah! Oh, men, here it comes – here it comes! Oh, shit, man, oh damn! Oh, gawd man, that feels so good! Oh, shit, man that is good! Oh, guys, thanks men, thanks! Oh, man what a feeling! Oh, shit, man, that was good! Oh, gawd guys – that was better than any jerk-off I've had in months! Oh, shit, man, thanks! Oh, gawd men, thanks – thanks!"

Slowly all three men regrouped from helping Randy shoot off, as if he hadn't done that for a long, long time.

"Oh, guys, oh guys! I can't believe this! I can't! Seriously guys, thanks for that! It's been a long, long time since I've had two hot built hunks like you two, doing something to me all at the same time. Oh, shit, guys, that was hot! Oh, man I love having two guys playing with me all at the same time. Oh, man that is so fucking hot! I love it, I love it!"

Then looking back and forth between the two, Randy grinned and then sheepishly asked, "Okay guys, gotta know! Which one of you two had your finger up in my ass? When you did that, that's when everything flew loose! When I felt that finger going up in there, that's when I lost it! Thanks – that really made it for me! Totally! Which one of you guys fingered my ass?"

Randy looked at Bill and realized that it obviously it was Jim, since Bill was standing there with his mouth hanging wide open.

"Looking over at Jim, Randy asked, "Hey, that was you, wasn't it? Jim, that was your finger up in there wasn't it?"

Looking at Randy with a big grin on his face, and again reaching around to Randy's butt and slapping it once, and then grabbing onto it, he admitted, "Yeah, guy, that was me! You got me so fucking turned on with everything that has happened here, that I just had to do that! Thank goodness you liked it! I was hoping it was okay if I did that! I mean, after all, by that time you had me so fucking turned on and horny myself, I had to do something crazy like that! Gawd I'm glad that was okay!"

Looking at Jim, and down at Jim's still stiff dick, Bill simply said, "Oh, really? Really got you all hot and bothered, uh?"

"Yeah, it did. Yeah, I gotta admit it did."

"I can see! Yeah, man, I can see! You still hot and horny enough to let me jerk you off, like we did Randy here?"

"What!? What did you say!?" Jim emphatically asked. What?"

"I wanna jerk you off! And maybe have you jerk me off if you want to. Face it man, I've wanted to do this to you for one hell of a long time. Come on, man, we've already been about as dirty and nasty with each other and letting Randy suck us off and playing with us as we can get! Come on – let me jerk you off! You just finger fucked Randy, let me finger fuck you and jerk you off, too!"

Looking at Bill, listening to him and what he was saying, and then looking down at Bill's hard on, Jim answered, "Okay, okay! Yeah, jerk me off. Yeah, I'll jerk you off too! Yeah!"

As Jim and Bill moved toward closer and closer – as each man reached out and grabbed the other man's dick – Randy said, "Hey, guys. I gotta get back to the pizza shop and turn the money in. I gotta go. You guys gonna do each other? You gonna jerk each other off?"

As Bill and Jim stood there with each other's dick in his hand, Bill looked at Randy and said, "Yeah, yeah, I kinda guess so! It looks like it man, it looks like it! Thanks man, thanks! Good job man – ya did a good job. I kinda think maybe you've helped us change some stuff here today! Thanks for everything! See you later!"

Randy grabbed his clothes, got dressed, and as he left the backyard, he yelled back, "Thanks, men! Had fun! Give me a call anytime! I'll help out anyway I can, anytime. Bye!"

As Randy left the backyard, Jim turned toward Bill and asked. "So what was all the thanking for? The fact that he gave us blow jobs, or what?"

"The fact that he helped me find out about you. He knew before he got here I wanted to see if I could play with you. Yeah, he came by once last year when I was swimming nude, but a little more than just that, happened then, and a few more times since then. I had told him about you, and he knew I was wanting to find out if I could do anything. After you shook hands with him, he looked at me and he saw me kinda shake my head, 'Yes.' Then he knew for sure, it was you. He played it so that if you weren't gonna do it, then it looked like I had no idea of what was happening. It worked! Come on, man, now I can say it – I want that dick of yours! I've wanted that dick of yours for years. Today, I finally get it!"

AT THE COMPANY MEETING

It was the much-anticipated annual company meeting week and Jimmy Stanson and Bill Morris were 'same company' employees, but Bill worked in Chicago and Jimmy was stationed in Cincinnati. Once a year the company had these "company wide meetings" for all of their managers, and the location this year was at an upper scale beach resort in South Carolina. The employees were treated very well. Wives were always included and treated to some very exciting and interesting events for their own personal enjoyment.

This particular day was Thursday, and Bill and Jimmy had only met on Monday of that week, but had quickly become rather close friends. They had mentioned that fact, a couple of times, and each man had rather agreed that since they were each new individuals to the company this year, that had become a bonding factor between them.

Bill was a distribution manager, and Jimmy was an area retail manager. Bill was 38, stood about 5' 10" and a man of rather average appearances, but Jimmy was definitely a man of many athletic abilities, and his body showed it! He was 40, stood 5' 11", weighed in at about 195 to 200 pounds, and had actually – no body fat! He truly did look like the man that probably every professional athlete wanted to look like. The face to lust over, and the body to die for! Even the straight and narrow type of thinkers would stop and get a good second glance at him whenever they saw him for the first time. Hot – really hot!

Bill and Jimmy did have a number of similarities between themselves, well – maybe bodybuilding was not one of them, and no wife on Jimmy's arm, could be called another major, major, difference.

Bill, Jimmy and Bill's wife, Janet, all had lunch together in the Patio Dining room, earlier in the afternoon, and Janet then joined the other wives in an afternoon of "A Guided Shopping Spree" in some of the unique upper scale lady's shops in the area. Since neither Bill nor Jimmy had any solid commitments for the afternoon, since the company had planned this afternoon as totally "free time," Bill had suggested that the two men meet down by the beach front at about two o'clock and grab some warm southern sun together.

Jimmy had agreed – "That sure does sound like a good idea," and did admit he was hoping to take home a little bit of a – South Carolina tan.

"Hey, tell you what!" Bill stated to Jimmy just as they were each headed out toward their rooms in opposite directions. "Come on up to my room when you're ready. We'll meet there then go to the beach, okay?"

As Jimmy approached the door to Bill and Janet's room, he tapped slightly and heard Bill say, "Oh, Jimmy, come on in. Come on in."

Jimmy opened the door, stepped inside, shut the door behind himself, and much to his major surprise, realized that Bill was standing in the middle of the room completely bare assed and obviously physically excited. He had his hand on a very firm and stiff hard-on!

Jimmy looked at Bill with some absolute confusion and asked, "Bill! What in the hell is going on here man? What's going on? What're you doing?"

"Oh, Jimmy, come here man, I gotta feel you man, I gotta. Please, please, Jimmy, I gotta! Please, Jimmy, please let me feel you and that body of yours! Please! Please!"

"What!? What did you say man, what did you say?"

"I'm so fucking horny right now, I am! I am man! After I came up here from lunch I was looking at some of the company papers, so I had the TV sound off, but then I looked up and one of those cop shows was on. You know the ones where the real cops arrest people? Anyway, when I looked up, these three really, really hot looking cops were giving this kid a pat down, and they were grabbing his arms, kicking his legs apart and kinda pushing him around some, and seeing that – it just got me all hot and bothered. Those cops were so hot looking and I think that kid liked it! I really do! I think he liked getting manhandled by those hot looking cops. I think he really liked feeling those cops putting their hands all over him and feeling him. Jimmy – when I was a real little kid, my Daddy had a cousin that was a policeman in town, and I loved it when we'd see him. His name was Les, and we'd stand on the street sidewalk and talk to him. I couldn't have been more than probably five or six and I loved to stand there and look up at him when he and Daddy were standing there and talking! I was little, and my face was right at his crotch level and I know, anyway I know now, I know I used to stand there and look at it right there in front of my face! Jimmy I've kinda loved cops ever since then. Oh, man, oh man! Oh, those cops, those cops on that show, they were all hot looking cops with tight, really, really, tight, tight, uniform pants on! Oh, Jimmy, their pants were hugging their asses and their crotches and their legs, and that kid, he was probably about twenty years old, and he looked like he really liked 'em rubbing their hands all over him! I know it probably had to be my imagination, but I swear once, one of those cops really groped that kid's crotch and rubbed and felt his dick and balls when he was feeling his legs for stuff! The kid wasn't mad at all – he was smiling. I didn't have the sound on, so I don't know what he was saying. But he looked like he liked it. Oh, man, seeing that made me so fucking hot man, so fucking hot! I wanted to be that kid with those hot looking cops feeling me up and down and running their hands all over me! I wanted one of 'em to be groping me!"

"Bill, I'm sure you've seen programs like that before, haven't you?"

"Oh, yeah Jimmy, yeah, but this time was different. Real different!"

"Different? Why was it different?"

"Oh, Jimmy, cause of you! Yeah – cause of you!"

"Cause of me!? Cause of me? Why cause of me? What do mean by that?"

"Cause I knew you were gonna be coming over here any minute, man. I saw 'em, and then I knew I was gonna have a man as hot as they were – right here in the room with me! Somebody that maybe I could get to feel me up and rub his hands up and down my body like those cops were doing to that guy!"

"But I'm not a cop man – I'm not a cop! So why'd you think of me? Why me coming over here get you all excited man?"

"Jimmy, cause of what you look like man! Oh, man, I could see you all dressed in a cop uniform like them! Yeah, I could just see you and that body of yours all looking like they did man – yeah I could! Oh, man, I could just see some really, really tight uniform pants on you and your ass showing off just sweet and nice man, real sweet and nice! Oh, Jimmy, you're gay aren't you? You gotta be gay! Please, please tell me you're gay, man, please!"

"I don't know what is going on here man, I don't!"

"Please, please just tell me you are gay! Jimmy, all I could think of when I watched those cops feeling up that kid on TV, all I could think about is, wanting you to do that to me! Please, Jimmy, please! Please, tell me you're gay, please!"

"Bill!? Bill, what if I am gay? Maybe I am, but you're not! You're a married man – married!"

"Oh, I know it, I know it! But all I could think about was wanting you to be one of those cops and you rubbing your hands all over me! Jimmy, ever since we met Monday, I've been really kinda attracted to you for some reason, and that show today, that just made me go over the edge. Honestly man, those cops and those tight pants and that one guy that had those big, big arms – they looked just like yours! They were big and strong, just like yours! Oh, Jimmy, things are so weird for me right now, real weird, but I've gotta tell you – I've wanted something like this to happen to me every time I remember back to when Daddy and I stood there on the sidewalk and talked to Les. I've looked at and I've watched policemen and cops, and highway patrolmen wearing those tight, tight, ball hugging, uniforms with lust – ever since then! Those highway motorcycle cops and their really, really, tight pants just turn me on, inside out! I don't know how they can wear 'em without ripping the ass out of 'em when they throw their leg up in the air to get on the bike! Oh, I get a hard-on whenever I see 'em do that! I always have man, I always have!"

As Bill stood there leaning up against the front of the room desk, trying to hold himself up from falling over in his light headed state of mind, he looked at Jimmy and again asked, "Oh, Jimmy, you are gay, aren't you? Please, please tell me you are! Please! I've gotta feel you and have you feel me! Please, tell me you are gay! Please, please I wanna feel you touching me and rubbing on me like those cops did to that guy on TV!"

"Yeah, yeah – I'm gay. But what's that got to do with what's going on with you? Bill, you're going kinda a little crazy here man. You've watched those cop shows before haven't you? You've seen cops frisk guys before haven't you? What's going on with you today?"

"Oh, yeah, yeah, I've watched 'em before! And every time I do, and every time I see some hot built cop in his tight uniform pants, with that fabric hugging his ass, and his crotch, I gotta make sure nobody knows how excited I get. Seriously man, if Janet's there, I gotta be real careful! Jimmy, ever since I've been a little boy, I've liked cops when they're wearing those tight uniform pants and shirts, and today, watching 'em on TV and then knowing that you were about to come over here – that just you and I were gonna be in here, all alone together – that just got me all turned on! Just watching those cops feeling that kid up just made me rip everything off and start jerking my dick! I was so glad I was here all by myself! I don't know what I would have done if Janet had been here! Jimmy, I've never had any kind of sex with a man before, but – oh shit I hope I'm not getting in big deep shit here, but man – can we do something? Please – please! Something together? Oh, shit, man! Oh, crap! Oh, please, can I do something with you? I gotta feel you, and feel you touching me! Please, man, please! Please, please – I gotta feel you, please man!"

Standing there, rather confused and bewildered, Jimmy looked at Bill, and watched Bill looking him up and down and often directly at his crotch, and slowly pondered his question. With about a full minute going by with neither man saying anything, Jimmy finally said, rather quietly and softly, "Yeah, yeah, I guess so. You sure you wanna though?"

"Oh, yes, oh yes! Oh, God yes! Oh, I've finally told some guy that I want to, and hell yes, yes! Yes I do! Oh, Jimmy, I've wanted to tell some hot looking guy like you for damn near my whole life that I wanted to do something, and I just couldn't until now! Oh, yeah, yeah! Please, man, please! Jimmy, I don't know what to do, but man, if we can, please, please, let's do!"

"Okay, if you want to – I'm game, but we'd better be careful! I don't want either one of us getting in trouble. Tell you what! You grab some clothes and get yourself kinda covered up some, and let's go over to my room. I sure as hell don't wanna be in here if Janet comes home, and I don't think maybe getting your bed all messed up is gonna sit very well with her either. I think we'd better go use my place, and be a little safe. If we got caught, we'd both be in big, big, fucking trouble!"

As Jimmy made his statement, he walked over to Bill, reached out, grabbed Bill's hard-on, and said, "Well, I can say one thing man! If you ain't never had this rod played with before, it sure is gonna have a good time this afternoon! I sure didn't think I'd be getting any cock this week but if you're game, I sure as hell am too! Specially with that big thing man – especially with that! You've got a hot rod man – one hell of a hot rod! Come on. Get some clothes on that'll cover that thing up, and let's go over to my room. You've got me all hot and bothered now, too! I sure as hell never expected anything like this to happen, but man, you've got me really turned on, and hot and ready to have some good, big cock, fun here! Real ready!"

Jimmy slapped Bill's stiff, thick, solid rod back and forth a couple of times then helped Bill find something to put on. Jimmy did strongly suggest that he do wear his swim trunks, so that, just in case they never made it to the beach, at least, he could come back to his room looking as if they had.

During the two and a half or three minute walk over to Jimmy's room, the two men had some very private, slight conversations about how often Bill had secretly prayed many times that something like this would happen. Something where he would finally have the opportunity to actually find out if having sex with another man was really as exciting – actually doing it, as he had always imagined.

Jimmy realized just how weird it felt to be walking through the resort, talking about having gay sex with another company person, and a person that he had just so recently met. And, also, with a man that had never had any man-to-man sex before! Somebody totally virgin to this type of activity! Right now, he felt kinda like some young kid talking about it for the first time, with some buddy of his.

After reaching his room, Jimmy suggested that Bill undress, and that maybe they should take a shower to get things started. He told Bill, "That's a good way for two guys to start feeling each other and kind of get some of the nervousness out of the way. And besides, I love to feel a man that's got good slick soap all over himself! You want me to feel you up all over, well I'm game, and that's gonna be a good way for us to get started."

The two men, now each carrying a stiff stick, both of which were bouncing up and down as they walked from the bedroom, went to the bathroom and both got into the shower. As Jimmy closed the shower door, Bill turned on the water and started to adjust it so that the temperature was just right.

Standing behind Bill, Jimmy placed both of his hands on Bill's waist. He then slowly moved his hands around to the front of Bill in such a way as to be hugging his waist.

Bill readjusted the temperature, and had his attention focused on that as Jimmy slid his right hand down the side of Bill's body and placed it toward the front of Bill's right leg, immediately under his erect cock.

Bill threw his head up into the air and let out a moan. "Oh, Jimmy! Oh, my gawd Jimmy! I had no idea I'd feel like this! Oh, my gawd man! Put your other hand down on the other side, please, please!"

Jimmy then slid his left hand down around to the front of Bill's leg and pulled himself up against Bill, as he grabbed Bill's left leg, once again immediately beneath the now raging, bouncing, and throbbing hard-on that Bill was supporting!

Jimmy's cock had gotten extremely hard as he reached his hands around Bill's body, and he had to flip it to a side, to get it out of the way, so that he could place his bare body up against Bill's bare backside.

Jimmy pulled Bill back tighter and tighter to himself, all the while sliding his hands up and down his body, feeling and enjoying the slippery slide of the soap against Bill's skin.

Bill moaned and dropping his head down as if he had lost control of his neck muscles, and he again moaned, groaned and exclaimed, "Oh, my God Jimmy! Oh, God Jimmy! Grab my legs! Oh, God Jimmy, let me feel your hands on my legs, man! Oh, let me feel you touching me, man, let me feel you! Oh, yeah, this is what I wanted, this is it! Just like the cops were doing to that kid on TV! Yeah, man, yeah!"

The water was flowing over the two men as Bill, for the very first time, enjoyed the unbelievable feeling of another man up against his bare body, and the ecstasy of having another fully grown man feeling his body, rubbing his hands up and down, along his legs, up and under his armpits and around front to feel his chest and slide across his nipples.

As Jimmy was squeezing Bill's body and pulling it up to himself as completely as he could, Bill was reaching around with both of his hands, attempting to grab ahold of some part – any part, of Jimmy. He wanted to touch Jimmy's bare skin, any skin, any place he could reach!

Suddenly Bill turned around so that he was face to face with Jimmy. He threw his hands around Jimmy's body and let each hand land firmly on Jimmy's butt cheeks. As he realized just where his hands had landed, he squeezed. "Oh, man! I've got your butt in my hands Jimmy! I've got ahold of your bare butt, man! Oh, God it feels so good, it's so tight! Oh, man, it is so tight! I've got your butt in my hands! I can't believe this!"

Jimmy had a hold of Bill's butt cheeks. "Yeah, I know man, yeah, I know! And I have your butt in my hands too! Oh, God Bill, your ass feels good! Oh, Bill, you feel so good to me!"

Jimmy hugged Bill's body, and started to lower himself down somewhat so that he could put his face on Bill's chest. Bill realized what was happening, and loosened his grip just enough to let Jimmy slide down, but yet held on firmly enough so that Jimmy would not collapse completely to the floor. Bill had realized that Jimmy was getting very excited too, and this totally unexpected excitement coming from Jimmy was definitely making Bill that much more excited!

Jimmy moved down to the top of Bill's chest. He laid his head up against Bill's chest and slowly started to tongue the hair on it. He moved it back and forth with his tongue! He sucked some of it into his mouth. He bit onto the hair that he had in his mouth, and very slightly pulled on it. He then asked, "Like this man, like this?"

Bill moaned, and lowly said, "Oh, yes man. Oh, my God Jimmy, nobody, and I do mean nobody has ever done that! Oh, my God! Oh, Jimmy – what a great feeling! What a feeling! Oh, this is great, simply great!"

Jimmy moved his head slightly lower and placed his face squarely in the middle of Bill's pecks. Jimmy buried his face as deeply into Bill's chest as he possibly could. He pushed his face up against Bill's chest so firmly that Bill had to quickly adjust his stance so that he didn't get pushed over. Bill continued to moan with pleasure – pure pleasures! He continued to hold Jimmy so that he would not collapse down, onto the floor, and continued to let him know verbally just how great this entire experience was turning out to be! He was adamant when he whispered to Jimmy, "Oh, man, I would never have thought it could be this great, just the feeling each other and being naked up against each other together. Oh, man, this is great!"

Jimmy moved his head to the right and took Bill's left tit into his mouth. All of a sudden, Bill was getting a tit sucking, and he let out an enormous moan of pleasure. "Oh, my God Jimmy! Oh, my God! Oh, God Jimmy, I have never – oh man, oh man! Oh, Jimmy, suck on that tit man! Oh, shit, man! Oh, my God, do it, do it! Oh, God! Oh, God, I had no idea that this could happen. Oh, suck on my tit man – suck on my tit!"

"Oh, God Jimmy, this is great! How long have you been playing with other guys? Oh, I know I'm not your first guy, but Jimmy, this is the first time I've ever done anything like this! Oh, Jimmy, you've done this to a lot of other guys, right? I can tell you really know what you're doing man, I can tell you've played with a lot of guys!"

As Jimmy pulled his face back just slightly, he looked at Bill and said, "Yeah, man, I've had my share, but you are great! Seriously, you are great! I never expected to have any fun like this while here this week! I'm gonna eat you up man – I'm gonna eat you up! Is everything alright with you man?"

"Oh, shit Jimmy, nothing could be better man! Oh, Jimmy! I am so damn glad you finally agreed to let me feel you and do stuff with you! Oh, this is so much better than I ever thought it could be! Oh, God Jimmy, I am so glad we're doing this. This is better than having sex with some woman, really it is! Oh, man! Oh, chew on me, man! Please, please! Oh, please just chew on me someplace, man, chew on me someplace! That is so fucking hot to me, man, it is! Yeah, yeah, do it, do it!"

Jimmy had already replaced his mouth on Bill's tit and was biting on it so very gently and lovingly. As he did so, Jimmy actually realized that all of his actions on Bill's body were not just "funny playing around." He realized, as he chewed on Bill's left tit, and continued to feel his ass and the crack in that ass, that he was actually making love to that tit, and not to just to the tit, but to the man! The whole man! 'This is not just playing!' Jimmy thought to himself. 'I am actually making love to this man! I'm loving him and his body! He is the one that begged for us to do this, and I'm the one that is now making love to him!'

Jimmy moved his face to Bill's right tit. Bill moaned as Jimmy sucked the tit into his mouth. Bill grabbed ahold of Jimmy tighter and pulled him up closer to himself! He grabbed ahold of the back of Jimmy's head and forced it onto his tit! As he did, he pleaded, "Oh, Jimmy, chew on my tit please! Oh, please, please!" As he begged and pleaded, Bill attempted to push his chest out toward Jimmy and his biting teeth! He wanted his tit bitten, and he was begging for it!

With their moving in the shower some, Jimmy was now getting a face full of water as he pressed himself up against Bill's furry chest, and chewed on his tight and firm tit. Jimmy chewed on Bill's chest and his tits, then started to lower himself down, lower onto Bill's torso. His face landed in Bill's navel. Jimmy pushed his nose in the navel, and then licked it with his tongue! Bill continued to moan in very accepting and exciting manners. He knew he was experiencing feelings that he had never before felt, but had, for many, many years, wondered about!

Jimmy slid his tongue out, and slid his face down, the full length of Bill's chest and stomach, down toward the top of Bill's fuzzy crotch. He placed some of Bill's fuzz in his mouth and pulled. He then went back to Bill's body and grabbed more. Bill moaned. He definitely liked the feeling of having Jimmy pull on his crotch hair with his mouth, and he loved knowing that Jimmy face was so very close to his crotch and his stiff rod, that was there, and definitely begging for attention.

Bill's stiff cock was right at Jimmy's face. Jimmy was hitting it with his face, and was rather playing with it by pushing it out of his way with the side of his face. He had not yet put his mouth on it, but he was moving it and rather playing with it with his cheeks, and his chin. He was having fun with it, and when he would push it down, it would fly back up and hit him in the face. He looked up at Bill and watched Bill break out into a very wild grin. He more than just liked the action that Jimmy was doing to him and to his dick! Never before had he ever had somebody playing with his stiff dick like this with even a hand, let alone the side of his face!

The way Jimmy was playing with Bill's stick of meat, made Bill get more and more excited. He realized that Jimmy had not yet actually touched it with either of his hands or his mouth, but just the idea that some guy had his face down there and was pushing it around with the side of his face and using his chin on it, was something that Bill had never thought could ever happen. Every time, when it flipped back up from being pushed down, that made Bill more and more excited about just what was happening to himself. New things that he had never felt before! Things that he liked and really made him get all excited about. He knew he was finally having some hot man-to-man contact! Contact like he had dreamed about for years! He was being played with by another man, one very, very hot and hunky man!

Jimmy buried his face in Bill's crotch hair, and very slowly let his tongue out just a little so that he could feel the fuzzy hair on the tip of his tongue. He did not know if Bill could tell that he had done that or not. In one way, he rather wanted to have Bill know that he had, kind of, touched his dick and his bag with his tongue, but then at the same time, he was not completely sure that he wanted Bill to know just yet, that he had done that. He knew he wanted to be able to see Bill's face when he realizes, for the very first time, that another man was licking or sucking on his dick, or his bag of balls. Jimmy realized that they were both getting very, very excited about all of this activity! Much more, than they were supposed to or had expected to, when they decided to 'just start' with a shower. He knew that they were supposed to only be taking a shower, and Jimmy had not expected to, personally, get so anxious and so sexually excited. He realized he was actually getting more excited than Bill was. Or anyway, so he felt! Being the experienced gay guy, he had truly expected this to just be another one-time, "fling in the hay." It just was not turning out that way!

As Jimmy pushed his face forward, he heard Bill say, "Hey, my man, stand up here, please! You've got me so damned hot, I need to get my face up against you, now! It's my turn to find out what that feels like. Here Jimmy, stand up, please! Let me lick on you some! I've gotta feel my tongue sliding on you! Jimmy I've got to see if doing it, feels as good as getting it done to you! Jimmy, let me at you, please!"

"Okay, yeah, yeah, man, yeah! Yeah, Bill – but let's go get in bed first! Bill, I never expected to get this hot playing with some guy that's never done it with a man before – but right now, I feel like some junior high school kid that's getting sex for his very first time! Come on, man, let's hit the bed! I've gotta get you man, I've gotta! Bill, thank goodness you got all horny watching that cop show! Let's get in bed and you can make believe that I'm one of those cop guys – all you want! You can feel me up – all you want! You can play with this 'cop guy' – all you want, and I'll do anything you want done in return. Come on man, I need you, and I need you bad! You are one hell of a hot man, and I'm damn glad you wanted this! Damn, I'm glad we were gonna go to the beach this afternoon! What a way to do a company meeting! Come on man, let's hit the bed and let you find out just how great having a man in bed with you can be! You've got me all hot and bothered, and now I'm the one begging for us to do some stuff together! Come on, it's time for us two company guys to get it on together!"

"JOHN, WHO WROTE THIS!?"

I was in the kitchen on the phone talking to one of my buddies when the front door bell rang. I ran quickly to the door and found out that it was my neighbor from across the street, Bill. I threw the door open and told him to come on in.

"Hey, Bill. I'm on the phone for a minute trying to figure out a hiking trip for this Sunday with a buddy of mine – so give me just a second and I'll be right there."

With me getting back to the 'hiking conversation,' Bill went on into the living room.

Not realizing just how long I had been on the phone, I finally did get it all figured out with Jack, and I headed for the living room, apologizing as I went for the longer than polite absence that I had given Bill.

As I rounded the corner going into the living room, I attempted to apologize face to face, but stopped in my tracks as I realized that Bill had picked up something, something that I had forgotten was on the coffee table, and he was reading it.

Looking up at me, and with a "Wow" look on his face, Bill anxiously asked, "John, who wrote this!? Is this something that you wrote?"

Stunned and kinda in a small state of shock, I looked back at Bill and said, or tried to say, "Oh, shit, man! Bill I forgot that was laying there!"

As Bill reached down and rubbed his crotch, he again asked me if I was the person that had written the story that he was holding and reading.

"Yeah, Bill, yeah. Yeah, but I really didn't mean for that to be laying out for you or anybody else to see. Bill, I'm sorry!"

As Bill again returned his attention to the page he was then holding he read aloud, "As Sammy was stretch out on his back across the sleeping bag, Tom took ahold of Sammy's ankles, pushed 'em up and over the top of Sammy's head, and with a very firm grip on his own eight and one half inch long dick, he aimed it right at Sammy's rose bud asshole, and went in! Sammy looked up at his hunky, muscular older cousin, smiled, licked his lips, and said, Tom, I love this man, I love this!"

"And this part over here on page two!!" Bill then exclaimed as he was still rubbing his crotch even more anxiously and grabbing for page two, to read, "As they each climbed out of the cool fluid of nature's streaming water, Sammy, the really, really hot looking 21 year old, muscled football quarterback, home for the summer from the State University, and his 25 year old, former State University wrestling champ cousin, reached out and, each man – one man at a time, grabbed onto the stiff and blood filled manhood rod of his cousin. Sammy stooped down, dropped to his knees and for his very first time, finally had the opportunity to see – really, really up close to his face and his eyes, and then grab ahold of, and then finally taste, his cousin's cock – as he had dreamt of doing, ever since the very first time they camped together – way back when they were young, small, and of course, small town boys. Sammy finally, and emphasizing FINALLY, had managed to get a very private camping trip set up that would be just he, himself, and the hunk of his dreams – his wrestling champ cousin Tom. This time it was not going to include either of the fathers, brothers George and Herb, nor any brothers. Just the two! Sammy, and in his mind, the hottest looking hunk on his side of the world, Tom!"

Then, Bill, my neighbor daddy, the daddy of three small grade school children, the husband of one very beautiful and smart wife, and the district manager of one of the most successful upper scale eating establishments in the area, looked at me, continued to even more vigorously grab his own crotch, and he almost exploded, "My gawd – I haven't been this fucking hot since I was a stupid teenager! John this part – yeah this part here – 'As Sammy leaned forward onto Tom's hard-on of a cock rod, and Tom then placed a hand on each side of Sammy's head and pulled his cousin's head forward so that he could force his exploding dick back into the farthest depths of Sammy's mouth, he then let all of his Kellinson family juices fill the depths of his cousin's throat, he locked the two family athletes together, and allowed his juicy warm milk parts of himself to invade the younger cousin.'"

As I just stood there, watching Bill scoot back and forth on the edge of the chair, continue to rub harder and harder his own crotch, and read from the page, he looked at me and said, "Oh, John, I am so fucking horny reading that!! I'm about to explode. I need you man, I need you to do something to me, or at me, or with me or something! Whatever, whatever!! John, please, please, please!! I've never played with a guy before, but John, please, please, can we go in the bedroom and do something? Please!? I've never been this hot man, I've never. Reading this is making me go crazy man, real fucking crazy!"

I was in total shock! Total!! I had known Bill and his family ever since he and Sharon had gotten married about ten years earlier, when I was 23 or 24 and had moved in across from them to remodel the house I now have, and at that time a house that really did need somewhat of a handyman to take it over. I manage a local hardware store. I do know how to do some handyman type of stuff! I can handle a hammer just as well as I can handle a dildo!

Bill and I had always had a very friendly friendship, and I certainly did respect his rather 'straight family lifestyle,' and I can only assume that he always knew I'd rather have guys around me than ladies, although it was never discussed. I kinda guess it was the "Don't ask, don't tell," type of relationship. Well, that was until today! It sure as the hell did look like maybe that was all gonna change! When your neighbor man is sitting there in your living room, rubbing his own cock as hard and as vigorously as Bill was, you just knew things were gonna change and be a little different than they had been!

As I stood there, for really the very first time, well maybe for the first time in a number of years, I looked at Bill with kind of a different eye. I was looking at him as maybe a playmate, and a rather exciting playmate, and I don't mean the kind you play baseball with. I did know he is three years younger than I am, so he scored a 31 there, and for a chest, he must have scored at least a 47 or 48, and that was above the waist that could not have been more than 33 or 34. As I stood there and now looked at him as a real living male species, and no longer just as 'the Daddy from across the street,' I started realizing that maybe that T-shirt and those 501 shorts he had, maybe slightly shrunk, or I was finally allowing myself to see what a real hunk I had living across the street, that I just had not been enjoying quite enough of. Arms to die for, and especially on a man that was not exactly a construction type of worker individual. Big strong tight biceps!

"Bill, Bill! You sure man, you sure? I sure didn't mean to have that layin' out here in the open for you to see. Bill, we're neighbors, and besides, you're a married daddy! The more I stand here and look at you, the less I wanna ask you if you're sure, but I don't want you doing something that you later regret! You're hot man – I mean it! I'd love to throw you on the bed and make whoopee with you, but I don't wanna do anything that you'll regret!"

"Oh, John! Yeah, I wanna! I do man, I do! John, I've known you were a gay guy the whole time we've known each other, I just never thought there was any reason to talk about it – until now! John, seriously man – this stuff I've been reading here, is that real stuff? Is that how guys get their dicks sucked on? Do guys really pull other guy's legs up in the air and fuck 'em in the ass that way? Is this really the way you guys do stuff?"

"Yeah, Bill, yeah! I guess I kinda assumed everybody knew that even if they're not gay and playing around that way. How far did you get, reading, before I came in?"

"Oh, man, I was reading about Sammy sucking on Tom's nuts after Tom fucked Sammy in the ass and shot off in him! Oh, man, please do that to me John, please! Oh, man, when I read how Tom slid each of Sammy's nuts in his mouth and then started sucking on him, I thought I was gonna bust a nut right then! Oh, I've been rubbing my nuts ever since I started imagining these two guys striping down and finding out they both had hard-ons on. That Tom guy was just as anxious to get to Sammy as Sammy was, wasn't he?"

"Yeah, Bill. See my story Tom guy, is a former state champion wrestler, and being able to grab ahold of guys, especially big hunky guys, and hold on to 'em and get his hands on 'em in some rather private body spots, was his real reason for being so excited about wrestling. It was a real turn on to him, to be in front of a whole gymnasium full of people and be able to reach up and under some hot looking hunky guy's big muscled ass and actually grab onto his dick and his balls! Yeah, Tom was as anxious for doing something with his cousin Sammy, if possible, as Sammy was for doing Tom. Until this day, it had just never worked out to where they were out in the woods all by themselves and could finally let each other know how horny they were for playing with each other."

As Bill did continue to sit there, squirming around in his chair though, and continued to look at the pages he had in his hands, or maybe I should say hand, since the left had was still rubbing his cock, he looked up at me and said, "Oh, John! When I read where Sammy was really scared to really let Tom know he wanted to do something with him, he didn't really know if Tom was going to want to do it, did he?"

"No, he didn't! He sure as hell was hoping though! Remember where Sammy called Tom and kinda wondered around in the phone conversation just trying to find out if Tom would go camping or not? He was really hoping his cousin would say 'yes,' but he was fucking scared he'd say 'no'. Sammy had never known for sure if Tom would play or not, and of course Tom never had any reason to suspect that his younger cousin was into it either. Hell, Tom figured Sammy was the State University Quarterback. He figured he was getting all the college girl pussy he could handle, never knowing that he was actually getting more football cock than pussy. Later in the story, farther back than you have gotten to so far, he tells Tom about all the football boys he's been doing ever since he got to State."

"So he's been wanting to play with Tom for a long time then, right?"

"Yeah, right! Yeah, right, and to be honest, I kinda think maybe you're in that same situation right now – right?"

"What? What? John, what do you mean? I don't understand."

"Bill, I never looked at you as a possible sex playmate, well until now that is, but now that we've been talking and I've been watching you rubbing your crotch so much, you've thought about wanting to play around for some time now haven't you?"

"John, I don't know! Really, I don't know! Maybe! Yeah, maybe. Yeah, John, I guess so. Okay, okay man, I'll be honest! You got some hot looking shiny gym shorts that you wear once in awhile, cutting the grass. Yeah, I admit, I've watched you some of the time when you have 'em on, and I've always kinda wondered what you had on under 'em. Briefs or maybe a jock? And yeah – yeah – then of course I'd wonder how big your dick was and if it might fall out or not. Oh, John! John, I can't believe I'm telling you this stuff! I can't believe it!"

"So big deal Bill, big deal! We're both guys! And I sure as hell am not gonna be telling anybody else about this, so don't worry."

"Oh, I know John, but I never thought I'd ever be telling anybody, especially you!"

"Especially me? Why especially me?"

"Cause man. It's your dick I was wondering about. A guy isn't supposed to wonder about another guy's dick!"

"Bill, it happens all the time! When you read in there about Sammy finally getting to look at Tom's dick up good and close, and how hard and stiff it was, and then about Tom grabbing onto Sammy's piece of meat, what did you think? When you read that, did that make you wanna lay that paper down and quit reading it? Did it?"

"No, hell no! John, that's when I got a hard-on! When they were touching each other for the first time, right after they stripped down to jump in the lake, they each got a hard-on, and so did I! That's when I was hoping you'd stay on the phone longer and not come in here! I needed to find out what they were gonna do to each other! I'd never read anything like that between two guys, any yeah, it made me horny. I'd still like for you and me to do something if we could. I mean man, I'll never tell anybody else that I got excited reading this stuff, and honestly man, my dick is hard and I need to either do something or go jerk it off! It's hurtin' man, it is."

As I stood there listening to Bill get all excited and telling me all excited about how he felt when he read about Tom and Sammy touching each other for the first time, rather unconsciously and really not knowing just what I was doing, I pulled my t-shirt up and off. Bill was getting me more and more excited just listening to him, and I guess I was starting to do the natural thing, and that was get ready for some good hot sex.

All of a sudden, I stooped down right in front of Bill, stretched out my hand, and allowed my finger tips to start the soft gentle journey up his left leg and up toward that pouch of hidden nuts and cock.

"Hey, Bill, find that part where Tom reaches up and slides his hand up inside of Sammy's leg and finally gets to kinda feel that hot little ass of his cousin's."

"Oh, John, here. You mean this part? 'Just as Sammy swam over toward the shore and started to pull himself up on the big flat rock that so many people used as a sundeck, Tom swam up behind him and so very gently reached out and touched Sammy's right leg right under his bag of nuts. Sammy stopped! He felt Tom's fingers feeling him on the inside of his leg, and he loved it. Slowly and lovingly Tom's fingers moved up ever so carefully and finally touched the bottom of Sammy's bag. Sammy let out a groan of total and complete pleasure! He loved it and he wanted to feel his cousin grab onto that bag of nuts and pull 'em back! Sammy laid there offering everything he could to his wrestling star cousin, and even begged for him to, "Grab me, man, please, grab my nuts! Squeeze my nuts Tom, squeeze 'em!'"

Now realizing just what I was in the process of doing, as I listened to Bill read how Tom had reached up and grabbed Sammy by the bag, I slowly did the same. As Bill read, I sat there directly in front of the hot crotch that I now had my hand moving up toward. Slowly as I listened and listened to Bill breathe heavier and heavier as he read, my hand moved up from the edge of his shorts, up and into the crotch area, where much to my surprise, I discovered no briefs nor jock strap! Only, but I should not use the word 'only,' one very stiff and abundant rod. As thick and unseen beautiful as it was and had to be, even though still hidden, there is no way a person could use the word 'only' in conjunction to feeling that dick! Hot as hell man, hot as hell! Now I was the man getting more and more excited and breathing heavier and heavier! It felt good, and I wanted it!

Bill looked up from the page, looked at me, and put on the cutest little puppy dog expression of 'Please, Mr. Master, please!' All of a sudden and honestly, without so much as even slightly thinking about what I was doing,

I pulled my hand out of Bill's shorts, jumped up, reached down, grabbed Bill under both arm pits and as quickly and as smoothly as if he only weighed ten pounds, had him standing and stripping his pants down and off of him.

With his pants laying down around his ankles on the floor, his dick sticking out at least nine inches from his gut, I grabbed the bottom of his t-shirt and actually stripped it off of his head.

"Oh, John my God man, I'm so fucking hot man, I am about to go crazy! Oh, John I've never done anything like this! Oh, man, oh man!"

I bent over, grabbed Bill's left ankle and helped him step up and out of his shorts, and then his right ankle. I stood up, grabbed him around the waist, hugged him up tight and then went for the tits! Bill stood there, now fully naked except for the gym shoes that he still had on, looked at me with his mouth wide open, put his hands up on the top of my shoulders took a big deep breath, and watched as I became the first man to ever suck on his tits.

"Oh, yeah John, oh yeah! Oh, yeah that's what Tom did to Sammy, and I wondered what it could feel like! Oh, John, suck on it man! Suck on my tit! Oh, yeah, man, oh yeah! Oh, John I can feel you on it man, I can feel it! Oh, it feels so damn good! Oh, John, suck on the other one man, suck on it too!"

I switched from his right tit over to his left tit and replaced my mouth on his right tit, with two fingers that love to squeeze a tight and firm tit, whenever possible. And this was a possible time! Bill's tits were tight, and firm! They were virgin tits, and it was almost possible to tell that without even asking. When any man reacts as much and as strongly as Bill did when I first put my lips on either one of 'em, that's a damn good sign that he's never had this done before! Just the sucking on 'em was a complete and total turn on to me! They tasted good! They felt good, and I could tell the more I sucked 'em into my mouth, the harder they got! Bill was being treated better than he had been for a hell of along time, and it showed.

All of a sudden I realized that I could feel two thumbs inside of the waistband of my gym shorts, and those thumbs were slowly moving down, and taking the shorts down with 'em.

"John, I gotta man, I gotta!"

"Do it man, do it!"

I did not wait for Bill to offer to help take my feet out of my shorts once they hit the floor. I immediately bent down, stepped out of 'em, dropped my knees to the floor, and ate his cock!"

"Oh, my gawd man – oh John – oh John!"

I had a mouth full, but Bill didn't except for his gasping for air and trying to yell "Oh, my gawd man – oh John – oh John," all at the same time!

All of a sudden, right in my living room, in the middle of the day, I was sucking on my neighbor that until only about ten minutes earlier, I would have never thought would ever be a possibility! I had Bill in my mouth and I had both of my hands grabbing his tight ass as strongly as I could. I don't know how in the hell he knew how to do it, unless he really zeroed in on some of the story line with Tom and Sammy, but he grabbed ahold of the back of my head and pulled me up against him as tight as the pigskin on a football! No other way to describe it – just as tight as the pigskin on a football! I was locked into place! Thank goodness I was not a newcomer at this! I had about nine inches of thick, stiff, steak meat rammed down into the back of my throat, and if I had not previously had my face, sat down on, by some 200 hundred pound plus men, and forced to eat their dicks without moving, I'd have never been able to survive this face fucking. Bill was way beyond just wanting to do something, he was now taking complete control! He force fucked my mouth, and I do mean 'force fucked,' about ten or twelve times the same way a man swings at a slab of concrete when he's trying to break it into small pieces.

He stopped, I pulled off about halfway, took a deep breath, grabbed onto his tight buns again, then pulled him back in! Once again, he had his hands on my head, and I was getting it in the mouth like a fucking jack hammer. I was having trouble trying to breathe, but I sure as hell was not gonna tell him to quit! It had been probably a month since I'd had a dick of this size in my mouth, and I was gonna take it and enjoy it like it was Christmas time.

After probably ten or twelve minutes of our 'getting to know each other' there in the living room, I just had to get him into the bedroom! Grabbing his butt muscles, and then slowly starting to stand up, I slowly slid my tongue up the center line of his tight muscled stomach, licking first the left tit and then the right tit, and softly said, "Come on man, I want you in the bedroom."

Leaving all of the clothes laying on the floor where they had landed, including Bill's shoes which he had managed to kick off, in-between the face fucking sessions, I led Bill into the bedroom where he had more unexpected surprises. On my bedroom walls are some full size posters of some pure muscle men – men that I love to look at as I often lay in bed and beat off.

"Oh, shit, man! Oh, John, they're hot man, they're hot."

As I slightly led Bill to the edge of the bed, I replied, "Yeah. Yeah, wish I was one of 'em, or at least could fuck around with one of 'em."

Now sitting on the edge of the bed, his nine inch rod standing stiff up in front of himself, Bill replied, "You know John. I've seen some guys like that at the gym before, and I will now admit to you, that I've often wondered just what it would be like to be in bed with one of 'em. Rock hard bodies like they have – gotta be a hell of a lot different than with a gal."

Just as I again stooped down right in front of Bill, grabbed his dick, and aimed it for my mouth, I quickly said, "Yeah, and I hope this is way different too!"

My arms went up beside Bill's legs, my mouth immediately went down on the inch and a half or three quarters, thick piece of meat, and I felt both of my tits getting pinched. I tried to utter a "Yeah, yeah," but with as much as I had in my mouth, I'm not just sure how well I did, in letting him know that he was catching on real fast! As I sucked, he humped up and down on the edge of the bed. I was getting a mouth full, I was getting my tits played with and I was not complaining!

Ten minutes of dick eating, or on Bill's side, face feeding, was enough to make Bill decide it was time for something else, another something that he had never done!

"Hey, John. In your story, Tom puts Sammy down on his back, grabs his ankles, pushes 'em up over Sammy's head and then fucks his ass, right?"

"Yeah, they each did that to the other guy, but maybe you never got to where Sammy finally gets into Tom's ass, did you?"

"No! No I didn't! Oh, John, I'm gonna have to read that part too! Hey, before I leave, can I read the parts I never got to?"

"Yeah, of course! I'd send the story home with you – but not so sure that would be a good idea, don't you?"

"I agree, I do. But, anyway John – can I fuck you like Tom did to Sammy? Can I do that?"

"Hell yes you can man, hell yes! I wanna feel all of that meat of yours going up in my ass! Hell yes! Let me grab some lube from the drawer, let me lube up my ass some and of course your dick some, and then all we gotta do is lay me down on my back, get you back there right behind my ole ass, you grab my legs, put 'em up in the air, find my asshole and then feed it! YES! Yeah, Billy, yeah! Hey, man, while we're fucking around with each other, okay if I call you Billy? I like calling you Billy while we're do the fun stuff, okay?"

"Yeah, man, if I can call you Johnny! Okay?"

"Hell yeah, man, hell yeah. Hey, tell you what! From now on, whenever I call you and you answer the phone, if I tell you this is 'Johnny' and I call you 'Billy,' that'll be our way of saying, I'm horny and I need you! Okay?"

"Yeah, hell yeah! Oh, shit, man, this is fun! John, uhh-I mean Johnny – of course you already know I've never had sex with a guy before, and today sure is a different day for me, but that idea of our 'Billy' and 'Johnny' is kinda fun too! I makes me feel like we've really got something going between us! It does!"

"Yes Billy, it sure does, and from what I am now feeling going up in my tight ass, I think maybe we've got something more than just the names going between us. Right now it feels like we've got ourselves a steam locomotive between us! How you doing man, how's that feeling to you?"

"Oh, Johnny, it's feeling good, damn good! But how far in can I push it? How far can I go? I don't wanna hurt you any, but I gotta tell you, from here, this is hot man, fucking hot! Johnny, can I push in some more?"

"Hell yes man! Hell yes! Put all of it in me, man, all of it! I've taken the whole damn thing down my throat a couple of times already, I want the whole damn thing up in my ass! Come on man, push it in me! Yeah, Yeah! Do it – do it! Now fuck the hell out of me, man – fuck the hell out of me! Fuck my ass like you fucked my face! Pound it man, pound it! Make mince meat out of it man, come on, pound it!"

With "Billy" up on his knees and his railroad car of a dick up in my ass, for almost a full fifteen minutes, he humped me, he pounded me, and he rammed me as hard as he possibly could! The sweat just flowed from his forehead down onto my face and my chest! He kept pushing my legs up higher and higher, and I kept offering more and more of my ass for him to use. How in the hell I ever thought I could offer more ass, I'll never know, but I wanted to give him all I had, if I had not yet done that! My ass was hungry, full, rammed and rammed, pounded and pounded, but I wanted and needed more! I just kept yelling at him, "Pound me, man! Pound me! Oh, Billy boy – pound on my ass! Use it man, use it!"

I really don't know how I can even use the term, 'all of a sudden' since my Billy boy had been beating his dick inside of me like a storm tornado on the go, but 'all of a sudden' Bill started screaming, "Oh, my God man, oh my God! Oh, John I'm gonna shoot man, I'm gonna shoot!"

He let that fly about three times, and I think each time he was a little louder – then all of a sudden – yeah once again that, 'all of a sudden,' but it was not! He stiffened up like a fallen oak tree trunk and shot about five enormous cum loads into my ass! I felt each and everyone! And on each and everyone, I yelled, "Yeah, man, yeah! Go man, go! Do it man, do it! I like it man, I like it!"

I was wasted, totally wasted, and my Billy boy was too! He flopped on the bed and gasped for air! Slowly and softly he tried to say, "Thanks man, thanks!" I knew what he was saying, well trying to say! He had no air! He still had a stiff dick, but no air. I told him to lay down and re-coup some, cause then I was gonna show him just how good it felt to be the guy on the bottom. He then tried to scream, "No, no!" But that didn't come out very well either!

Bill looked over at me and again and again he tried to tell me he couldn't get fucked in the ass, and again and again I looked at his face each time he tried to plead 'No,' and each and every time I could see the real plead of, "Yes, oh yes please, but I have to keep saying no." I heard him say, "No," and at the same time, I saw the face of a man that really, really did want it.

"Hey, Billy guy. Lay still there for a minute. I wanna go get that story from in the living room. There's a page or two I want you to read while I freshen up in the shower, okay?"

"Yeah, okay, yeah."

I grabbed the story and then found the section that I wanted Bill to read while I took a shower. I handed it to Bill and told him, "Here, read this. Think you might find it interesting."

Starting from the page that I had handed to Bill, he read:

Tom spread Sammy out, gut down on the sleeping bag and told him to, "Lay there and open up that ass, cause your ole cousin is gonna eat you out and then he is coming in!"

Tom grabbed ahold of each side of Sammy's ass, pulled the cheeks apart, and actually threw his face down just as deep into that hole as he could! Tongue sticking out and flipping up and down in anxiety, Tom was finally – FINALLY, eating out Sammy's ass! Pushing his face in as hard as he could, he licked and slurped on that hole and its rim as strongly as he could, and stayed there eating and licking for at least fifteen or twenty, exciting and tasty, minutes.

Sammy was in heaven and he kept telling cousin Tom that he was finally getting what he'd been praying for! Over and over, he kept begging, "Oh, Tom, Tom! Eat it man, eat it! Yeah, man, do it, do it! Lick my hole man, lick it! Stick your tongue up in me, man, come on farther man, farther! Oh, Tom eat me, man, eat me!"

Tom went after that ass stronger and with more gusto than any ass he had ever gone after.

For years and years he had been wondering just what it would be like to eat out the State University's star quarterback, but never thinking there was any possibility – until that grateful day two days earlier.

It was only two days earlier when cousin Sammy called and asked if maybe he'd be interested in going camping with him over the week-end – in a real, back and out of the way, kinda secret and private place that he had found out about. The words, 'real back and out of the way, kinda secret and private place,' were the magic words that made Tom's dick stand straight up, as he tried to stay calm and let his younger, hot muscular football star cousin know that, "Yeah, man, yeah! Hey, Sammy guy, I'd like that, I really would! You and me, just you and me, right?"

He got the answer back that he was praying for, and it was, "Yeah, Tom, yeah! I thought it'd be fun if just you and I spent some private time together out there in the woods, maybe swimming naked in the lake, or doing whatever we wanted, and just enjoying ourselves together! So yeah, man, just you and me! Okay?"

As Tom pushed his hard-on down and kinda back and forth some, the idea of him and his hunky cousin spending some nude time together, 'swimming or whatever we wanted' was a true and glorified present for Tom to hear and to re-say to himself over and over for the next forty eight hours, and then of course during the really anxious two hours, riding in the jeep together, sitting so close together, side by side, just getting to the fabulous, 'real back and out of the way, kinda secret and private place!'

The two hour drive, sitting that close to the hunk of meat that each of the men wanted, but still didn't know if it was gonna happen, if it could happen, or even how to find out if it could happen, was rough. Tom was driving, and Sammy was watching. Yeah, watching Tom's crotch almost constantly! He was hoping that his prayers were gonna be answered, and he had no idea at all that Tom was thinking the same thing! Two horny guys – one close together jeep ride, and two hours praying was making it a rough trip. Only once during the jeep ride did anything get said, that even came slightly close to what both of the hunks really wanted to talk about, and it was Sammy's comment about his dormitory roommate and how well he was built. Then in fright that maybe he was gonna say the wrong thing and Tom would just turn the jeep around and say, "Hey, bud! I think maybe this camping out together thing might be the wrong thing for us," he stopped, and never added anything to it! He knew he wanted to tell Tom about fucking his roommate, and he wanted to tell Tom about how big of a dick his roomy had, but he knew he'd better just shut up and not push the envelope any! He knew he just had to wait for just the right moment to let Tom know that he definitely walked on the man side of the street, and not the pussy side. And it happened just about one half an hour after they got to the lakeside – threw down their sleeping bags – stripped off their shirts and shorts, and Sammy got caught looking at Tom's growing hard-on.

"Hey, man, you looking at it is making it get hard! It's not used to being looked at! Don't look at it Sammy, don't!"

The prize was there! Tom was getting a hard-on, and that was the slight simple clue that Sammy needed, to give him the guts to 'go for it'!

"Hey, Tom man, I gotta, I gotta! Tom, I've wanted to see your dick and watch it get hard ever since we've been little guys. Every time you were wrestling some other big hunky muscled guy, I was the one sitting there trying to hide my hard-on, cause I wanted to be the one you were grabbing in the crotch and throwing around! I wanted it to be my dick and my nuts you were grabbing onto! Come on man, let me touch it, let me see how it feels! Come on Tom – please man – I wanna feel it and I want you to grab mine too!"

"Sammy – Sammy – you serious man!? You serious? Sammy you trying to tell me you play with guys!? Sammy – is that what you're saying man, is that right!?"

"Yes, hell yes Tom! Hell yes! Please, please tell me you'll let me kinda play around with you while we're out here! Please, Tom, please!"

"My God man – Sammy I had no idea! You're the big football star quarterback! Sammy, you starting to tell me that maybe you're playing with the football boys more than the cheerleaders!? Sammy, is that what you're saying man?"

"Yes Tom, yes! Tom, I'm gay! I'm fucking gay! Please, Tom, please don't be pissed at me, please! Tom look, your dick is as hard as mine is right now, see? Tom please, please tell me you play with dicks too, please tell me! Please, don't be mad at me – please!"

Tom reached out, grabbed his cousin around the shoulders, hugged him tight, and said, "Hey, Sammy I'm sure as the hell a long way from being pissed – I'm ecstatic and happy as hell! Sammy, me too! Sammy, I've wanted to fuck that tight looking ass of yours for one hell of a long time! I hope like hell you get fucked man, cause I want it, and I want it bad!"

"Oh, hell yes man, hell yes! Tom I get fucked and have been getting fucked since high school! Tom, the whole reason I wanted us to come out here camping this weekend was cause I wanted to do, whatever I needed to do, to get you to fuck me! Oh, man, I was praying and have been for years that you were gay and played around with guys and would fuck me! I just couldn't ever get anything arranged for us to be alone someplace together where it could happen.

Oh, Tom – yes – hell yes I want you to fuck me as long and as hard as you can! I need that dick man, and I need it bad!"

And now the time had come! Tom grabbed some lube, smeared it on his dick and on Sammy's anxious asshole and then got in position to take what he'd been wanting for a hell of a long time. He was finally gonna get to fuck his cousin's ass, and he was gonna enjoy it just a much as Sammy was gonna enjoy getting pounded with his nine inch rod.

Just as Bill had reached the spot where Tom was finally gonna get to fuck Sammy, I walked back in the bedroom and watched Bill look up at me and smile.

"Oh, John, you think maybe I can? Shit man, after reading that and seeing how much Sammy was wanting Tom to do him, maybe I can. I'm not sure, but I know you sure did like it when I was fucking you! Let's try, but if I can't, you won't force me to do it will you?"

"No, hell no Bill! Having sex is for having fun, not getting mean about it. Tell you what. Why don't you run in there and take a quick shower and kinda wash your dick off some, and then we'll kinda do a little 69 funning around here on the bed to kinda get you all in the mood. We'll play with each other like Tom and Sammy did in the story, okay? I wanna suck on that dick of yours some more and eat that ass of yours too. Ever since we got this started today, I've been anxious as hell to stick my face back there right between those ass cheeks of yours and see just how far up in your ass I can get my tongue. That Tom guy did it to his cousin Sammy, and that's exactly what I wanna do to you! Wanna see what it feels like to have some guy eat out your ass and do some good ole chewing back there?"

"Oh, my gawd John! Oh, shit, man – you've got me so fucking horny and turned on right now I don't know what I'm doing. Oh, my dick is so fucking hard right now! John – you're gonna suck on my ass? Is that right!? You're gonna put your face right up in there between my ass cheeks? Oh, shit, man, oh man, we gotta do this, we gotta!! Yeah, man, yeah, I wanna feel that man, oh yeah – I do! John I can not believe we are doing this stuff with each other. Shit I wish we'd started doing this stuff years ago! This is so fucking hot to me!

Oh, man I can't believe we've lived across the street from each other for ten years now and all that time you been over here doing this stuff with guys! Oh, shit, man, I wish I'd been over here too! Oh, man, what a hit! Oh, shit, man, you're gonna suck on my ass? Right!? You're gonna stick your tongue up in my ass just like Tom did to Sammy!? Oh, shit, man, I can't believe this!"

"Hey, Bill – go jump in the shower for a minute or two. I wanna eat that tight little ass of yours man, I do! I gotta eat it out good and deep! And I'm gonna try and do it deeper and better than Tom did to his cousin Sammy! Okay? Okay?"

THE PHONE CALL

"Hey, David! What you doing, man?"

"Oh, hi, Jimmy! Sitting here reading the nastiest, dirtiest, raunchiest, filthiest, sexiest stories I can find. I'm so fucking horny this morning, I can't stand it!"

It was only about 6:30 in the morning, and as David was – to his own admission, reading sex stories on the computer, the call had come in from his close friend, Jimmy. Both Jimmy and David were single gay guys, and although good and close friends, not the type of friends that could make it together as partners. David was definitely the, "go out and find it – and find it often," type of a guy, where Jimmy was much more the homebody type of a guy that liked gay sex, without question, but just not the road rage way that David did.

"OK guy! Why in the hell are you so horned up this morning? Didn't you get any last night?"

"Yeah, I did Jimmy, and I swear that's why I'm climbing the fucking walls this morning! I got it last night and I want more of it today!"

"So tell me! What'd you get last night? Who'd you play with? What'd you do?"

"Oh, Jimmy, I was with some fucking hot guy that was staying down at the Ramada that says – he's from out of town."

"Well – why'd you say – he says he's from out of town? You kind of make that sound like you don't think he is. Right?"

"Yeah, I don't think so! I think he is one closeted case that is scared to death that somebody, like maybe the city, will find out about him."

"The city!? What'd you mean by that?"

"Personally man, I think he is a city cop, or maybe a highway patrolman and he is so damned afraid of being found out about, he rents motel rooms for his action and then says he's from out of town."

"Why do you think that? Why'd you say that?"

"Oh, shit, man, just the way he was. The body to die for! One fucking hot and hung muscle guy that could and should be in any and every gay magazine so every horny guy could jerk off just looking at him. I'd guess he was like 35 or 36. Dark black flat top and facial hair that just puts his face in a fucking frame. A chest on him that I swear even the Pope would kiss and suck on! Tits – oh shit, man – how in the hell can I even describe those tits!?"

"David, how'd you meet this guy? How and where'd you guys meet?"

"Jimmy, believe it or not, a note on the fucking restroom wall at Stormy's! Yeah – a note on the partition in the restroom! Believe it or not man, a fucking note! Never have I ever thought some note in the restroom of some bar would ever pay off!"

"David – a note? You called some number written on some restroom wall?"

"Yeah, yeah, I did! I was at the bar and had to go take a crap. So I went into the restroom and took the first place. I dropped my pants and sat down. As I was sitting there, I saw this note written on the door with yesterday's date on it. It said something like, 'Horny top. Need tight ass tonight after 10. Local motel. Be cute, ready and very hungry.' Then, the phone number. It was a direct line into the room – oh! No,– no! You know what? That had to be his cell phone! Oh, shit Jimmy! That had to be his cell phone number! I called him directly, no motel answered! Crap, I never thought about that! Hell,

I never even thought about it being something different than a motel number! Shit man, I've still got that note! God! Oh, shit, man! I still have that number!"

"Well David, what happened when you called it? Who answered? Did he answer right away?"

"Yeah, Jimmy, yeah he did! When I called, he was kind of quiet and I could hear noises in the background, like he was not in his room. He asked why I was calling. I told him I read a note that had that number on it. He said, 'OK. So tell me about yourself.' I told him I was 27, six foot one, hundred eighty five pounds, and I had a hungry hole like he was looking for. Then he asked me if I got fucked very often. I told him, 'Yeah, but not as often as I'd like.' Then he asked me how big of a dick had I taken before. I told him I really wasn't sure how big the biggest one was, but that I used some pretty big dildos on myself, so I was pretty sure that whatever he had, I could take it. Serious Jimmy, I've never been questioned like that before, when I was trying to set up something. Hell man, I had no fucking idea of what this guy was like at all! Hell, for all I knew was he could have been some freak that nobody would ever go to bed with."

"Well David, if you knew he could have been some kind of a freak, why in the hell did you agree to go meet him? Why'd you do that? You are really gonna get your ass in real trouble someday with some of the guys you tie up with, man!"

"Jimmy, he was getting me all fucking turned on just by the way he was talking to me and asking me all these questions. Just the way he kept asking me these questions about what kind of sex I've had and who I've done it with was really a big turn on! It was like I was being interviewed for a radio program or something! Hell man, just being on the phone with him I was jerking on myself! He got me horny as hell just talking on the phone!"

"So what happened then? You guys – I guess – made arrangements? I mean, I assume you went to him if you guys played, right?"

"Yeah, right, but before we got off the phone, he made me tell him about the best ass fucking that I'd ever had. He wanted me to tell him about me getting it in the ass from some other guy. He wanted to hear about some other guy fucking me. So I told him about the time that I got pulled over in Missouri and the cop that stood me beside his cruiser, pulled my pants down in the back, and right there beside his car, pulled his big black dick out, and fucked my ass while I leaned on his car. Oh, shit Jimmy, I could tell just by listening to him, he was just about to pass out just listening to me telling him about that cop and that night! He kept asking me more and more detail about what happened, and about that cop and what he did to me. He asked me why I got pulled over and I told him, that as far as I knew, it was because when the cop went past me earlier, I looked over at him, and he looked back at me. I had noticed that when he looked back, he started to grin. And I grinned back! All that guy on the phone could say right then was, 'Oh, fuck man! Oh, fuck!' Jimmy, he was cumin in his pants right then, I know! The way he was sounding on the phone right then, I know damn well he was either jerking himself off – if he was someplace to do it, or he was at least making a mess in his briefs."

"Oh, shit David, what'd he say then? What happened?"

"Well, after I heard him take about three big deep breaths, he asked me if I'd ever been tied down or handcuffed when I got fucked. I told him, 'Yeah, both. I'd been tied down – all fours, a couple of times when I was with some guy I trusted, and yeah, over at the play house I'd been handcuffed a few times when I was chained to the wall so that guys could come and either feel me up or maybe ram me. Once again I could tell he was just about ready to have a fucking heart attach! Hell man, I was wondering if he was gonna hang in there long enough for us to even get together or not. I could hear him huffing and puffing like crazy."

"David – you have been chained to the wall so guys could fuck your ass? You never told me that!"

"Yeah! Hell, I figured somebody would have told you! Hey, not trying to keep secrets from you buddy, but hell, I figured Joey or Rich would have told you by this time. Hell man, Rich is one of the guys that chained me up there the last time. Sorry – just assumed you knew!"

"OK, OK! So now I'm really starting to find out just how fucking wild you can get, I guess! I knew you were really into some different stuff, but never knew you got yourself all chained up to a wall so you couldn't move any. Not surprised – just finally having some more stuff admitted to me. So you and this guy last night! I have to assume you did more than just the phone stuff right?"

"Oh, fuck yes! God Jimmy, he had me so fucking horny before we finally got off the phone, I was messing up my briefs too. Well – anyway would have been if I'd had any on. Sure did mess up the cut-offs though! After the phone call, I noticed that I had this nice little wet spot down there."

"Yeah, yeah! For you that's nothing new! You do that all the time! Tell me about the other guy! What happened next?"

"He kept asking me about that cop in Missouri. He kept asking me over and over if I meant he was a black officer when I said he pulled his big black dick out! I had to tell him probably three times that, 'Yes, he was a black officer, a big black officer!' Then he kept asking me how he was hung – that black officer, that is. He kept asking me if that was the only black man that I had ever been fucked by, and I told him, 'No, but he probably had the biggest black dick that I had ever had rammed up in me!' He kept asking if that was the only cop I had ever been fucked by and of course I told him, 'No.' I told him I have a couple of local young and hung cops that stop by my place once in awhile when their wives are all pissy with them and they need some ass. I told him I get one or both of them at least every other week. I told him I kind of think they might like my ass better than doing their women. Man, oh man! That fucking idea really turned him on! About all he could do was ask, 'Local cops!? Local cops!?' Then he wanted me to tell him about them. I told him some sexy stuff, but nothing that could let him know who they were – just in case. I told him about how one of them was hung like a fucking stallion, and the other guy's dick was fatter than a coke can. I told him how the fucking stallion guy gets all the way up inside of me, good and deep, and how the coke can guy really pulls my ass open, big and wide, just to stuff it up in me. I could hear him huffin' and puffin on the phone all over again! Then like all of a sudden, he had to do something, and he quickly asked me if I could come by his place at 10:30. I told him, 'Yeah, but I have no idea of where.' He told me to recall the same number after 10:00 and he'd give me the address. Now I was really getting all excited. Some guy I had no idea about, but sounded sexy as hell on the phone, and now some location that I wouldn't know about until just before I headed there! This was getting really exciting! This was really turning me on man – in a big way! The fact that he got so fucking turned on about the cops thing was really turning me on!"

"Oh, shit, man, I can not believe the life you live. So, what then? You just waited till ten and then called him again?"

"Hey, I wondered the whole rest of the day if this was gonna be some kind of a standup deal, and when I called again, if he'd say he changed his mind of something. It was about three o'clock when I found the restroom note and called him. So for about seven hours, I had to wonder if I was gonna be taken for a ride, or was I really gonna get to let this guy take a ride on me."

"Hey, David – the note! After you took his number, did you leave the note there or erase it?"

"Oh, at first I just left it there. Then after talking to him, I went back in and erased, it so nobody else could find it. I thought, fuck man, I don't want any competition on this one. About nine o'clock I started getting ready. I did the enema thing and made good and sure everything back there was all good and cleaned out for some good ass fucking and hoping, maybe, some good ass kissing, and then started deciding what to wear. Decided I wanted to look as sexy as possible. I decided I really didn't want to wear a shirt, if at all possible, but since I still didn't know where I was going to, decided to at least wear a tank top and maybe my leather vest. I put on the tightest fucking pair of Levi's I have. I wanted the crotch on them to show more than I probably have. Hell man, I even thought about using an agile sock, for show."

"Oh, shit David! I've played with that damn thing before, and hell man, I've even had it up in my ass a few times! You sure as ass hell, do not need some argil sock stuffed in there beside that fucker. Unless you've cut part of it off since I've last seen it, I'm sure it showed quite nicely! Especially – if you put on some fucking tight Levi's. Hell man! Your crotch shows a basket when you've just got dress slacks on! With that fucker, you sure don't need anything extra! Ok – so now back to your mysterious playmate! Hope like hell, that if he fucked you, he had as much to use on you as you could use on him – or – maybe the fucking got turned around. Did it?"

"Hey, man, one step at a time here now. OK? Remember I hadn't even met this guy yet! Hell, for all I knew, when I got to wherever I was going to, once I took a look at him, I might have wanted that sock so that I could take it out and throw it at him."

"But I'm guessing that's not quite what happened right?"

"Oh, hell no! Shit no! I called right at 10 o'clock. He answered right away. Everything behind him was quiet this time. I could tell he was someplace different than earlier in the afternoon. You know, I never thought about that until now. You know Jimmy, now I'm sure that was his cell phone. I'll bet he didn't even have the motel room yet when I talked to him in the afternoon. God – man I'm stupid! I never figured that out till now."

"Hey, David, don't slap yourself around over that. From what you've been telling me, I'm not so sure I'd have thought this all through either. I kind of think you were getting so excited about all this that you just never stopped and thought it through. So – OK – you called – then what?"

"Well, I called and this time he asked who was calling. He didn't do that earlier. Earlier he asked why I was calling. So anyway I told him I was David Packard and that we had talked earlier in the day. Then he asked, 'What did we talk about?' I told him we talked about me getting fucked by some cop in Missouri. Then he said, "OK! Just needed to be sure you were the same guy. Told me he was in room 217 at the Ramada and to show up at his door right at 10:30. Not before, not after, right at 10:30 – even if I had to sit in my car and wait for 10:30. I told him, 'OK', and then I asked him, 'Was there anything I needed to bring with me?' He asked if I had those dildos handy that I had mentioned earlier in the day. I told him, "Yeah. Want me to bring them?' He said, "Yeah, but make sure they are well hidden and could not be seen." I told him, 'Ok,' but Jimmy – I have to admit, that even I, don't usually go walking around with a handful of dildos showing."

"Yeah, got to admit that's kind of a funny statement, isn't it?"

"Yeah, I thought so, but you know, I still think it's because he's so afraid of being found out about, that he didn't stop to think that no guy, gay or straight, is going to be walking around with a handful of dildos showing."

"I guess. Yeah, I guess maybe so. So I assume you showed up right at 10:30?"

"Yeah, I did. With my sack of dildos in hand, I waited until right at 10:30 then knocked on his door. I heard him ask from inside, 'Who's there?' I said, 'David, David Packard.' I heard him unlock the door, it swung open, but nobody was there. Well, didn't look like anybody was there. I stepped in, and the door closed. I turned and was face to face with God! Believe me, man, this was one hell of a lot more than I expected! I'm serious man, to me he was God! Like I said earlier, something out of some gay magazine that everybody would swear was a computer made picture. Jet black short flat top, a day's beard growth, at least six foot three, probably 230 pounds of nothing but solid muscle and a thick uncut dick, sticking straight out, that had to measure minimum ten inches long and at least seven inches around! I didn't get to measure it, but I've had others in my mouth, and up in my ass to judge it by! Jimmy, you know me well enough to know I've had a lot of dicks stuck down my throat and run up my ass, right? Well this was the biggest one I've ever played with before. Jimmy, you've been fucked by Big Billy before, right?"

"No! Hell no! No – I saw that damn thing hard one time and there was no way in hell I was gonna let him get close to my ass with that thing! No, David! No! I have never been fucked by that monster. No!"

"Oh, I figured you had. Hell man, I think every other gay in town has been. Hell, even those guys that always claim, "I'm only a top," have taken that one. Well anyway, this guy was bigger, both in length and in width than Big Billy's is. I'm serious Jimmy, I choked like a dieing chicken when he put that damn thing in my mouth!"

"Oh, shit David, what happened after you went in? After the door closed? I assume he was standing there behind the door, right?"

"Yeah, he was. Totally bare assed naked, and totally fucking unbelievable! His rod was standing out like a fucking flag pole! He did not say a word. He reached out – took hold of my vest – took it off – grabbed my tank top, and literally jerked it off of my head! Undid my Levi's, and pushed 'em down! Well, of course, I had a major hard on then too. Hell man, as soon as I had my first glimpse of him. I was raging hard! He reached out and grabbed around my dick and my bag. He pulled me forward, which made me stumble since I now had my pants down around my ankles. He still did not say a word! He put his hand on the top of my head and pushed. I knew immediately what he wanted. The best I could with my Levi's down around my ankles, I knelt down, and immediately started on that rod! Oh, shit, man – what a fucking rod! I've always said I can take any sized dick down my throat – right away, and without choking – well, I used to say that, until last night! Now, I now my limits!"

"Hey, David! This guy! Does he have a name? Did you ever find out his name? Did you guys ever talk to each other, or just suck and fuck?"

"Hey – Jimmy. I don't know! I really don't. He told me to call him "Butch," but I will be totally honest with you and tell you that I have no reason to even think, that is his real name. And to be real honest – I guess I really don't care! When you get a chance to play with probably the hottest body within in a hundred miles, why care about the name?"

"Well, yeah – got to admit, yeah! So, did you finally take all of his dick?"

"Yes, I sure did! In both ends! My jaw is sore today, and I still feel like my ass is standing open getting ready for some locomotive to go driving up in there! And I kid you not, even with the dildos I use on myself, that fucker last night felt bigger than that biggest dildo I have. And Jimmy, that big dildo I have, has got a head on it bigger than my fist! One day when I sat down on that damn thing, I wondered if I was taking more than when I get fisted. So after I took it out, I measured it, and then measured my hand. And that fucker is fatter than my hand. So, even though I can't fist myself, and yeah – I know some guys can, at least I can use that "Big Tony" on myself and feel like I just got fisted. Hey, you know a guy's gotta take care of himself, once in awhile, right?"

"Jesus, David! Have you tried putting the fucking dinning room table up in that ass of yours yet? God man, is there anything you will not put up in your ass!?"

"Well, shit, man! You know me well enough to know I'm not anything even close to what somebody could call vanilla! I need more action than that! Hey, remember that day you helped me plug myself with that butt plug, that I just bought and couldn't get up in my ass? Don't tell me you don't know I'll try anything! Hell man, I got all excited over a fence post once. Didn't do it! Was afraid I couldn't get up off of it if I took it, so had to walk past it, but sure didn't want to! That day, that was one fucking hot looking fence post, let me tell you!"

"OK, OK! So what are you doing right now? Besides telling me about your God given man, and what you two did last night – what you doing right now? I know you can't be reading the stories on the computer anymore. What you doing while we're talking? Fingering your ass? Jerking you dick?"

"Hell, yeah, man – hell yeah. Both! Yeah, I have been ever since I started telling you about Butch! I'm sitting here bare ass, grabbing my dick and my balls, jerking on them like they were jerked on last night, but shit, it don't feel the same, and I'm pinching and squeezing my tits as hard as I can, like Butch did to me, but it don't feel the same either! God man! Every time he touched me, anyplace, it was hot and exciting! Oh, man, I've never had sex like I did last night!"

"So what else happened beside you trying to take his dick while you're kneeling there with your pants down around your ankles?

"Oh, shit Jimmy! After I got my shoes and Levi's off, and only about half of his rod down in my throat, we moved over to the bed. He laid down on his back and let his human baseball bat stand up there – like some major league flag pole! Shit man, I thought it looked big when he was standing up, but fuck man, when he laid down and that damn thing was standing straight up in the air, it looked twice as big! Jimmy, I choked and choked on that fucker. I'm serious! I've never tried to put that much in my mouth before! He laid there for probably half an hour and just let me take it a little bit at a time. I finally, and I do mean finally, took most of it! He let me do my thing, and he never tried to force me onto it. I'm sure he's had a hell of a lot of guys that have tried and tried and maybe never got as far on it as I did, so I guess he was happy. Or hey – maybe I was the first guy to even try it! Jimmy, I wouldn't be surprised if last night wasn't that guy's first time with a guy. He sure came across as if it could have been. God if so, I'd sure like to know for sure, that I was the first guy to take his fucking big dick down my throat and up in my ass too!"

"So, I assume he did fuck you, right? Oh, what a stupid question! God, how could I ask such a stupid question? Hell man! The way you are talking about this guy, if you'd been laying on the railroad tracks with a train coming, you'd still made him fuck you, so hell yeah – I know he finally fucked you! How'd it go? Hurt any?"

"Hey, man, do me a favor. Take two coke cans, one on top of the other and let somebody ram them up in your butt real fast, and then tell me if it hurt any. His dick is just about the same size as those two cans together, and hell yes man, it hurt! It hurt so bad, I want it again today! I know, I know! When he was on top of me and got that thing all lined up, I knew damn well that when it popped in it was gonna hurt, but Jimmy, I wanted that man up inside of me so badly! I would have taken twice that much pain to know he was up in me! Yeah – it hurt at first, but then it was the best fucking I had ever had! The first thing he said to me – the first thing since I got there – was when he was on my back and was up in my ass, and he told me to tell him again about that black cop in Missouri that fucked me up against his cop car! He kept telling me to tell him more, more! He told me to really, really tell him about that Missouri cop and how he was build, like about how long was his cock, how did it feel up in me, and every little detail about him and his body that he could ask! He told me to tell him about the local cops that come over and fuck me, he wanted to know if either one of them were black officers, and he wanted to know what they did to me. How they fucked me. He wanted me to give him all the details about what positions we used, and did the two guys fuck the same way, or what did they do different. Did I suck on them? Did they cum? Was the big long dick bigger than his? He wanted to know again if the big long dick was a black cop, and I had to tell him again – neither one of the local cops were black men! He really, really wanted to talk a lot more about some black officers. I know he was hoping that the local guy with the big long dick, was a black man! He wanted to know if I liked that real thick dick. He wanted to know if either one of them had ever sucked me off! He wanted to know if they know each other? Did they both know the other guy comes over and fucks me? He wanted to know if I had fucked either one of them. When I told him yeah, I had fucked both of them, then he wanted to know if they both liked it and did I know if they got fucked by other guys. When I told him I knew at least the one with the real thick dick did, he wanted to know if I knew if it was another cop that fucked him. I had to tell him, I didn't know. Wished I did, but didn't. He asked if I was the first one to fuck either one of them. He wanted to know if getting fucked out along the highway by that Missouri cop was fun and exciting for me! He just kept fucking me and asking me questions. I could kind of tell when I told him something that really turned him on. He'd slam my ass like he was using a jack hammer on an old sidewalk. Oh, fuck man – did he ever fuck me! Really, when I was talking about fucking and getting fucked by those cops, I think he was putting himself in my place. I really do think he replaced me, with himself. The cop with the really thick dick must have really turned him on! He kept asking and asking about that dick and what it felt like! He wanted to know what it felt like in my mouth and what my ass felt like when he opened me up and forced it up in me!"

"So David, what did you tell him when he was asking those questions? Did you tell him that it was fun and exciting to get fucked by that cop in Missouri?"

"Oh, hell yes! Yeah, man, I knew that the way he was acting, that if I told him that was hot to me, and that, that big black officer had the normal big black man rod on him, that was really gonna make him hot all over again. Hell, I remembered how he reacted on the phone earlier when I told him. I thought, hey man! I've got him and his fucking big rod up in my butt this time! Of course I wanted to get him all turned on! But hey – it was no lie anyway! The night that happened was fucking exciting for me. I couldn't believe it. When I saw those cops lights flashing at me from behind, I couldn't figure out what in the hell was going on. But then, when we pulled over and he got out, I looked in my rearview mirror, saw that big hunk of a crotch sticking out, and then I realized, that was the same cop that I had smiled at, and he smiled back. Thank goodness we were in some small town under the street lights when we passed each other, or I'd never been able to see him looking at me. Anyway, when he was pulling me over, I was really hoping this was not going to be a legitimate traffic stop. Hell man, as soon as he walked up to the side of my car, I started looking at that enormous crotch in those tight pants and made sure he knew it. He asked for my license and while I was getting it out, he reached down and moved his dick. And when he moved it, he had a lot to move! I know damn well he made sure I saw it! He kind of let his hand hit it a couple of times and I could see it getting bigger and bigger in those tight pants. Damn I wanted to just reach out and move it! I thought shit, man – if he can keep hitting his dick, then I'm gonna rub my own, and I did! He saw it! I licked my lips! I know damn well he took that as a, 'Yeah, I will!'"

"I purposely kept looking at his crotch while he read my license. His dick kept getting longer and longer! The head of it started showing through! He looked at me and I looked back. I know my face was not more than probably 18 inches away from that big crotch while I was sitting there looking at it! I know I had this, 'Come get me – do me,' look on my face. He moved his dick again, then said, "Come on. Get out of the car. Step over here by my car! Put your hands on top of the car!' I knew damn well, I had not done anything! Well, anything worse than kind of coming onto the cop. That was coming onto the cop, and then being pretty straight forward that I was game. I knew he wanted to play somehow, and hey, I was willing. – I was wild game – and I wanted him to know that! I put my hands on top of the car, he pushed me toward the car, reached around, unbuttoned my Levi's, slid the back of them down, made a small comment like, 'Good, no undies,' then I felt him reaching in between us and pulling his rod out. God, how I wanted to reach back and grab it, and to this day, I still don't know why in the hell I didn't!"

"He had some kind of a little tube of lube in his pocket and I felt him smear some on my hole. Oh, man! I pushed my butt back on his hand when I felt it touching my ass! That's when I should have just reached back and grabbed onto his dick! I was hoping he'd put his fingers up in me. Then, all of a sudden, I was getting fucked all the way! All at once! I didn't even know he had lined it up yet! All of a sudden, he was all the way up in me! No way in hell did he take any time! God man he nailed me fast! He slammed that fucking rod of his up in my ass with one great big fucking push! I hugged that cop car! I dropped my head down on top of that cop car and I kissed it, I did! I dropped tears on that car! I screamed – well anyway, I wanted to scream as loud as I could, but I just grunted and moaned! I laid my head on that cop car and wined. I'm not ashamed to admit, I wined. My ass felt like he tore the whole damn thing open. I thought God, I hope I'm not bleeding back there! Pretty soon the big pain stopped and all I could feel then was his big rod up inside of me, and his uniform being pressed up against me. Oh, God man! Oh, shit, man! That was so fucking hot! I could feel the front of his legs pushing up against the back of mine, and I could feel his shirt buttons and all the stuff in his pockets pushing on me. I could feel his belt buckle hitting my back every time he pushed forward! Oh, man! What a fucking hot fuck! I'd never been fucked by a cop fully dressed before! I had never had an officer's uniform pressed up against me and my bare butt! Shit man, what a great feeling! I'd do that again anytime, anywhere. Next time I really don't even care if it's daytime or nighttime out there! There we were, only a few feet away from the highway – and cars flying by at about 70 or 75 miles an hour! I've always wondered if any of them ever had any idea that some guy was getting his ass fucked out there, right beside the highway, up against the patrol car, by one of their own hot, hunky and damn well hung highway patrolmen. You know Jimmy! I do think one person did know, though. An eighteen wheeler honked as he went by. I'll bet he was up high enough, so that he could tell the cop was leaning on me and he probably knew that cop was really fucking the hell out of me and my ass, while it looked like we were just standing there! He might have been able to see us long enough to know that cop had his rod slammed up in my ass! He might have been able to see the cop pumping my ass back and forth! Hell, maybe he's seen other cops, doing some guy's ass, out beside the highway, using the cruiser as his leaning post before! Probably made him jerk off in the cab of his truck while he was driving!"

"God David, how did that all end? Crap man! I've got to admit, this is getting me all hot and bothered! I've never been fucked by a cop before, but shit, man, this is sounding pretty hot, even to me! I've never thought about some guy getting fucked, by some uniformed hot cop, while standing out beside the highway, and with cars driving by! Man, I've got to admit, this is pretty fucking hot sounding! What happened then? He didn't give you a ticket or anything, did he?"

"No, hell no! He knew I was really into what was happening. He knew I was really wanting this! He knew from me grinning back at him in that town that I was gonna be good game for him. That's why he got back behind me again, and then pulled up and pulled me over! He knew I sure wasn't gonna be any kind of a problem for him! I kept telling him to fuck me more, and fuck me harder! Once he told me, 'I'm fucking your little ass as hard as I can kid! I'm trying!' Then, without warning, all of a sudden, it hit! He shot his fucking patrol wad up in my ass like a fucking cannon shot! God, was that a hot cum! I mean really – it was really warm hitting up inside of me! All of a sudden, he dropped his head on my shoulder for only probably a few seconds. I think all of a sudden he realized where we were, and maybe he was afraid that somebody might stop, thinking something was wrong. He gave me one more big body push, and said, 'Don't ever say a cop can't fuck whoever – whatever and – whenever – he wants!' Then he pulled out, tucked his sausage back in his hot tight uniform pants, well anyway, tried to. He was still partly hard and had trouble getting it all tucked back inside. Hell, I still don't know where in the hell he put all of it when he got it back inside. He pulled my Levi's back up, and told me to button them up."

"You mean that's the way that whole thing ended? He just pulled out, you guys got redressed and that was it?"

"No, no, I didn't say that! We kind of got ourselves all put back together again, and then I just kind of, slightly, happened to mention, that I was staying at a St. Louis motel that night, and if he should just happened to be close to that motel that night, I sure would like to be pounded and rammed some more, and make him happy again, but in a little more private space. He looked at me and broke out in a great big broad smile! That told me he was maybe gonna do it! I gave him my cell phone number and told him to call when he got close to the motel, and I'd tell him which room I was in."

"Oh, shit David, I never knew this! Fuck man, you never told me about this happening! Did he come to the motel that night?"

"You know what he did? He got on the police radio – and signed off for the night! Then turned to me and said, 'Let's go kid! I'm done for the night, but I'm sure as the hell am not done with you!" We drove to the motel and he just let his patrol car sit there all night. Shit man! I only got about two hours sleep that whole night, but I will say, I probably got more fucking done in that one night than I usually get during an entire month! God, I love Missouri State Patrolmen! They are hot and can fuck like a rabbit! Well, anyway that one could!"

"David, what was this cop like? How old was he? Was he well built?"

"Yeah, he was hunky and had a good build. He was built like a cop is supposed to be. You could tell he did one hell of a lot of weightlifting. Told me the next morning he was 42, married, had his own secret 'boy' that took care of him, and he took care of the boy. But of course his wife didn't know anything about the boy! Said he's been married for 20 years, and has had his boy toy for ten of those years. Tells his wife he needs to be at the station on nights when he never goes home. So taking the whole night to play with me was no problem. Said I reminded him of his boy a lot, except that I was white and kinda looked like a loaf bread to him. Told me my ass was tighter than the boy's. Figured over the years he had probably stretched his boy's ass open with all the stuff he stuffs up in there. Told me, he won't let the boy do anything except give him ass and suck him off. Told me the boy's not allowed to jerk off. He's only allowed to shoot off when he's in his daddy's ass! Said he was punishing the boy for not doing one of his friends right, so he needed to find some ass out on the highway till he went back to fucking the boy. He had told the boy he wasn't getting any fucking from his daddy for three weeks. Told me that's why I got fucked. He hadn't had any boy butt for about three days and was in a real need! I told him I was glad the boy had been bad. Turned out good for me! I sure enjoyed it!"

"Oh, shit, man! Did you tell that Butch that? Did you tell him that cop came to the motel with you and about him having a boy toy?"

"Oh, fuck yes! Oh, hell yes! I knew that if I told him that, he'd probably try to just craw up inside of me. I do not know why, but him hearing about me getting fucked by cops or sucking on cops, makes that man fucking wild! And the more I talked about my black Missouri Highway Patrolman, the hotter he got! Fucking my ass when I was talking about the black man, I thought was gonna give him a fucking heart attack! And when I told him about that cop having his own boy toy, I thought he'd faint! He looks like a cop, built like a cop, and I think he is a cop, and he wants to either fuck another cop, or get fucked by one. And honestly man, I think he'd go across country to either fuck a black cop, or get fucked by a black cop! He is just plain cop crazy! I wonder what in the hell would have happened if I had told him I was a cop, or if I'd even told him one of the local guys is a black cop! He probably would have eaten me alive or he'd have fucked me to death!"

"David, you took your dildos with you. Did you guys ever do anything with them? Why did he want you to bring them?"

After we kind of got all done, well kind of after he wore my fucking ass out and made it black and blue from fucking it so hard, I asked him why he wanted me to bring 'em. He kind of stumbled at first then he admitted that when he told me to bring them, he was then kind of wanting to maybe try one up in himself. He actually told me that while he was talking to me on the phone that day, he was sitting there and watching a man across the room that was sitting with his legs kinda open, and he was showing a big basket, and that was making him think about maybe taking one of my dildos up his butt! He admitted that that guy's big crotch was kinda making his ass squirm some, and then kinda quiet like, he told me that guy was a black man, and he really was showing one hell of a big basket, and he was wishing he could have seen just what was inside of those pants. But, after all the fucking he had just done, he wasn't so sure he could take one. He told me that when I mentioned them on the phone earlier in the day, that really got him all hot and excited. I told him, I'd help if he wanted to, and he decided, no. What he did do – which shocked the hell out of me was – first he asked if any of my dildos were black dildos, and I of course told him, "No, no they're not." He admitted then, that if one of 'em did happen to be black, he was gonna ask if it'd be OK for him to take it out of the bag, and just kinda handle it, and play with it in his hands, for a few minutes. Then he asked me if I happened to have any black dildos at home, that I just didn't happen to bring with me. I had to tell him, "No, no I don't." Then the second thing he did was, he asked, "Hey. Can I have your phone number so I can call you sometime soon? And then, before I fuck your ass, maybe we can try one of your smaller dildos on me. OK?" I damn near fucking fainted! I was in complete shock! He wanted to be able to call me! I looked at him and said, "Hell yes you can have my number! And, I kinda think maybe I oughta see if I can find a big long black dildo, before we get together again, right? Want me to do that?"

With one great big smile on his face he answered, "Yeah, yeah, if you can! Yeah, that'd be fun! Real fun!"

"Jimmy, I'm serious, I never thought about me having his cell phone number. See, I was thinking that was a motel number. I wonder if he's hoping maybe I will call him sometime. You think maybe he wants me to call him?"

"My suggestion to you is – do not loose that number! And go buy a black dildo, but I think it better be a pretty big one! Give him a few days to see if he calls you, then if not, call him and just remind him you read his note at Stormy's, and you still had his number! Be straight forward and just tell him you want to finish what you guys got started at the Ramada. Tell him you made a purchase! Hey – keep checking out the stalls in Stormy's too! He might post a new message. He might post a message asking for a cop, and don't be surprised if it's asking for a black cop! He probably wants to find your two local cops too! Hey – maybe you can get a four way set up!"

"Oh, my God Jimmy! Oh, shit, man! Oh, what an idea! Oh, would I be on top of the world then! Oh, man! My heart is beating like a fucking base drum! Jimmy! Gotta go man! Man, I've got to get myself all cleaned up! I've just made a mess all over myself here. Hey, let me talk to you later, OK? Bye!"

"Hey, bye David! Congrats on last night, and maybe tonight, too!"

YOU NEED A FRIEND

This day was not Danny's greatest day of his life and he damn well knew it!

Danny was a very smart and sharp guy, one month short of being 22, and hurting like he had never hurt before. One week earlier, Jeanne, his lady friend for the past three years had all of a sudden found herself a new man of interest, and dropped Danny like a bomb shell! Total surprise! Danny had had no idea at all that she was stepping out on him, and finding her "true love," in some old flame of a guy that she used to date when she was in high school!

Now one week later – to the day in fact – Danny had now just been told that his best buddy, Todd, was calling from Kansas City, and that he had taken a new job in Kansas City, and would be moving in one week! Slam bang! Crash bang! One, two –Danny was feeling like he had just been hit by an eighteen wheeler and with all eighteen wheels!

Losing Todd was probably hitting Danny harder than losing Jeanne! Danny and Todd were buddies from back in the junior high days – were the same age – had both been on the wrestling squad – had both been to state level competition – and had been more like brothers than just friends for the past nine or ten years! The damn dreadful phone call he had just gotten from Todd, hit him harder than Jeanne's admission that she'd been seeing her old flame for about the past six months!

His feeble attempts of trying to sound good and happy about Todd's success in getting the new job, was a little more than just a little hard to do. He put his cell phone in his pocket, stamped his foot, swung his hand in the air at really nothing, and then just let out a loud "Damn it! Damn it!"

His frustrations and his all of a sudden anger at being where he was, doing what he was doing, and actually at just about everything else he could manage to be mad at, he headed out the door and stomped down the street. He needed to get out of the house and just go for a walk to try and figure things out! Two really big hits, and all within one week, were just too much to handle without some level of total frustration, high frustration!

For an hour or even maybe an hour and a half, Danny had been out walking, looking down more than up, stamping the sidewalk more than just walking on it, ignoring every person that happened to come walking toward him, and suddenly realizing that if he had been only about five feet farther out into the middle of the street, they would have been putting him in an ambulance, if the hood of that car had not just carried him away!

After the street scene, or whatever you call the almost connection of an unprotected person and a forty mile an hour SUV, Danny did make the conscious decision that he needed to go someplace that did not have city streets and fast moving vehicles. He turned and started walking into Celebration Park, and did manage to get himself and his rather stupefied, empty mind, into a safer place.

The afternoon had turned to evening, and the trail lights in the park had turned on, and Danny did finally see something of "joy" or appreciation when he noticed the reflection of the lights shining back at him from the surface of the water in the stream that the path did follow. Finally, he stopped, took probably the first deep breath that he had had, since he talked to Todd on the phone, and he then sat down on one of the benches facing the stream. His posture was not bright and crisp, but obviously much more like that of a man that had just been told he was loosing, for the second time in one week, one of the most important people in his life! He was pissed, mad and lonesome!

All of a sudden, without warning, a man of about six foot two or three, and about 220 pounds plus, sat down on the other end of the bench, kinda leaned forward some, leaned his elbows on his knees, looked over at Danny and said, "You're not looking very happy guy!"

Shocked and rather surprised, since Danny did not even know anybody was close by, looked over at the man, and just uttered, "Yeah!"

"I've been watching you ever since you came in the park man, and I could tell something's not quite right. What's wrong man?"

Rather slowly looking back over toward the man, Danny quickly thought, 'Wait here man – just what in the hell is going on here? All of a sudden I'm sitting here, brooding in all my sorry stuff, and then this great big black man, that I have never seen before, sits down beside me and wants to know what is wrong? What's going on here?'

"Just some shit, man, just some shit! I'm just pissed, that's all."

"Yeah, guy, I can see that! I sure don't know what you're pissed at, but I sure can see you need someone to talk to and someone that you can spend some good time with, right?"

Now looking over at his new visitor, Danny sternly asked, "What!? What!?"

Sticking out his rather large hand, but a hand that definitely did fit the man that owned it, he said, "Hey, man, I'm Jake – Jake Corley."

Being very confused, but not wanting to be rude, Danny did return the hand shake and replied, "Hi, I'm Danny Davidson."

Without really realizing it, but before finishing the handshake, Danny did look down at their hands since he had just experienced this tremendous feeling that his entire hand had just been encased in this man's enormous paw!

After finishing the handshake, Jake leaned back onto the back of the bench, put his hand up on the back, over toward Danny, and then said, "Okay man, what's wrong! Tell me."

Still feeling damn confused and bewildered, Danny did feel just a little more comfortable and at ease since this enormous size of a man was acting so calm and friendly, he did answer, "Girlfriend and buddy problems! She dumped me a week ago, and I just found out a little while ago that Todd, my buddy for the last ten years took a job in Kansas City and is moving in a week. I feel like everybody is deserting me."

"Uh, wait here a minute man! Kinda confused! Your girlfriend? Right? Your girlfriend?"

"Yeah, yeah. Jeanne. She and I, so I thought, were probably gonna end up getting married, but she and her old boyfriend are back together and have been for about six months, but I never knew anything about it!"

"And your buddy that's moving, he was – – ?"

"Well, he was just my buddy. We went to school together, we were on the wrestling team together and hung out together a lot. That's all. A buddy!"

"So you're saying, you and he were just friends, and you and she were the lovers, right?"

"Yeah! Yes! Yeah, what'd you mean by that?"

"Uhhh, Danny, I kinda assumed maybe different."

"What do ya mean different? What are you saying?"

"Danny, do you know where you are?"

"Well yeah, I think. This is Celebration Park, right?"

"Yeah, it's Celebration Park, so I just kinda assumed, since you're in this part of the park, maybe I just assumed!"

"Assumed!? Assumed what!?"

"That you were gay."

"GAY!!?? Why in the hell would you assume that?"

"Danny, this is the real gay part of the park. This is the place guys come to when they're feeling kinda down and out and wanting to find a friend. When I saw you coming in, that's why I watched you. You're hot man, real hot!"

"Hey, man, I'm not gay – I'm not gay!"

"Well man, we never know! Yeah, I know you say you're not gay, but then – hey – things do change!"

Looking over at Jake, with one very confused expression on his face, Danny asked, "What!? What are you saying! What in the hell are you saying!?"

"All I'm saying is – once in awhile we kinda change the 'who we are' and the 'what we do.' Hey, maybe there's a good reason you happened to end up here today! Maybe something's guiding you here. What do you think?"

"What do I think!? What do I think about what!? What in the hell are you asking man, what!?"

"Hey, Danny, you're in a really bad mood today, right? Feeling kinda really low and alone, right?"

"Yeah, yeah of course! Lost my girlfriend and now my best buddy, what in the hell do you think?"

"I think you need company, you need a friend. Which hurt worse? Losing the girl or losing the buddy?"

"Losing Jeanne or losing Todd? That what you wanna know?"

"Yeah, yeah."

"Hell, I don't know! I thought Jeanne and I would probably some day get married, so yeah, she was pretty damn important to me, and Todd – hell it was kinda like we were married. We did everything together man, everything! Yeah, he and I have been like together for probably ten years or so! Yeah, losing him is gonna hurt a lot! I guess Jeanne, I'll find some other gal, but don't think I can replace Todd – nope – I don't think so!"

"So you and Todd. You did everything together right?"

"Yeah, yeah we sure did!"

"Sex?"

"SEX!? You mean Todd and me!? That what you're asking!?"

"Yeah, yeah. Sure. You said you two did everything together!"

"No we never had sex! We're not gays!"

"Ever wished you could? Ever wished maybe that you two could?"

"Oh, hell man! You know guys! We've got sex on our minds all the time!"

"Ever mention it to him? Ever tell him you wanted to?"

"Hey, man! I never said I ever wanted to! No – I of course, never told him I wanted to! No!"

"But you did want to, didn't you? You already told me guys have sex on their minds all the time. You said you two were wrestlers, right?"

"Yeah, yeah we were. In high school."

"Ever wrestle with him after high school?"

"Yeah, a few times, just for the hell of it. Just to kinda relive our high school days."

"Relive what about those high school days? The feeling him up against you and you feeling him?"

"No man, no! Just the fun of it, that's all."

"Oh, okay, if you say so!"

"Yeah, yeah I do."

"Buy Danny, tell me if wrestling him was still a lot more exciting for you than wrestling the other guys you wrestled. It was, wasn't it?"

"Well yeah – probably so. He was my buddy and we were always close. Yeah, wrestling him was always good!"

"You're gonna miss that once he's moved, aren't you?"

"Well hell yeah! Yeah, I'll miss a lot of stuff about him."

"Think he ever wanted to have sex with you?"

"What? Why in the hell would he ever want to have sex with me? He had his girlfriends too. I'm sure he had sex with them, he didn't need me for that!"

"Hey, Danny. When you two wrestled, did he ever grab you in the crotch a little more than some of the other wrestlers?"

"Yeah, yeah. Yeah, he did. And I used to grab him there a lot too. It was our way of just goofing off, that's all!"

"Did you like it?"

"Like what? What grabbing him?"

"Yeah, grabbing him, and him grabbing you?"

"Well yeah. Yeah, I liked it cause it was our way of goofing around with each other."

"You ever maybe grab him a little longer and maybe a little stronger than necessary?"

"Yeah, of course I did! I was getting back at him for grabbing my nuts once in awhile."

"Oh! So he grabbed you like that too, uh?"

"Yeah, of course! It was our goofing around."

"So Danny, tell me something. When he grabbed onto you like that, that ever make you get hard?"

"Yes, hell yes! When you have some guy grab your dick, of course it's gonna get hard!"

"Did his get hard when you grabbed his?"

"Yeah, of course it did."

"So tell me about his dick getting hard. Was it really hard and stiff?"

"Yes it was. Todd's got a big dick, well I guess cause it's bigger than mine, and so anyway I've always thought of his as being kinda big, and yeah, when it was hard it felt big."

"Ever see it hard? I mean bare. Out of his pants?"

"No, well not real hard. I did see it once when it was kinda hard, but then he hid it and I didn't get to see it anymore. He grabbed his shorts and put 'em on."

"Were you wishing you could have seen more of it?"

"Yeah, yeah I will admit I did cause since his is bigger than mine, I wanted to see just how big it gets."

"Here, reach over here and feel mine. See if you think it was bigger than mine."

"What!? What feel your dick!? Is that what you want?"

"Yeah, man, yeah! Come on, I want to know if you think Todd's dick is bigger than mine. Come on."

"Hey, man, I don't go around feeling other guys' dicks! No!"

"But Danny, you did like feeling Todd's right? You kinda said you did. You liked that right?"

"Yeah, but that was Todd! I don't even know you!"

"But Danny, maybe we need to change that! Come on man! Here, I'm gonna scoot over closer to you, and all I want is for you to put your hand on my dick, and then see if you think mine or Todd's is the bigger. Don't be afraid or anything. I'm not gonna bite. Besides, you're in the gay part of the park, and this kinda of stuff goes on in here all the time."

Jake did scoot over right up beside Danny, and as he did, Danny did look down at Jake's crotch.

"Yeah, man, good going! Right here, just put your hand right here. Come on man, come on. Come on, you admit you like grabbing Todd's dick – so feel mine. You might like it too! Come on, just for a second, okay?"

Jake put his right arm around Danny's shoulder and as he slightly gave it a slight hug, he again encouraged Danny to reach over and feel his dick.

"Hey, man, look at it. It's starting to push my shorts up some. If you don't touch it pretty soon, it's gonna poke its head out of the end of those shorts, and then I'll have to poke it back in. Come on Danny, just put your hand on top of it! Yeah, man, yeah! Yeah, Danny, yeah! Yeah, just let it lay there and let me feel it on my dick. Hey, how's that dick feel compared to your buddy's dick? Is mine bigger or is his?"

"Oh, shit, man! My God man! Your dick is big! Jake, your dick is a hell of a lot bigger than Todd's! Shit man, this thing feels like it's about twice as big as his! God man, Jake – this fucker feels like a telephone pole! Holy shit, man – this thing is fucking big!"

"Hey, Danny, mind if I feel yours? Can I feel yours?"

"I guess! What the hell, I'm sitting here feeling yours, I guess you might as well!"

"Oh, Danny, you got a nice dick too, and guess what! It's hard! How long you been sitting here with a hard-on man, how long?"

"Well it started getting hard when I reached over there and felt yours. I ain't never felt some other guy's dick before, well except while wrestling and then it was usually just Todd's. We like to kinda goof off grabbing each other's dicks and squeezing 'em."

"Want me to pull mine out so you can see it?"

"Jake, not here! You can't do that out here in the park can you?"

"Well, I shouldn't! Yeah, I could get in trouble if I did. Hey, tell you what man! My apartment is only about four minutes walk from here, let's go over to my place and then I can pull it out and let you see it. Okay? Let's do that, okay?"

"Oh, I don't know man, I don't know!"

"Hey, Danny, just to let you see my dick! Nothing else is gonna happen – but I like to show it off to guys whenever I can. I like for guys to see it! Come on, we'll just go over there and then I know I won't get in trouble by pulling it out here. Come on, let's go."

As Jake stood up, he re-positioned his dick in his shorts and definitely did notice that Danny very interestingly watched as he moved it to the side and rather tucked it back in. He said, "Come on, let's go."

Rather automatically Danny did stand up and started walking beside Jake without saying anything.

During the walk out of the park and across the street toward Jake's apartment, Danny did continue to express that he thought he was doing the wrong thing, but Jake kept reminding him that after having the kind of day and week that he's had, he really did need to be around somebody, and not be alone all by himself. Slowly Danny did kinda agree, and did admit that as crappy as he felt, he was kinda glad that somebody had paid some attention to him, and that he did have someone to talk to. During the short walk to the apartment, Danny did find out that his new friend, or at least his new acquaintance, was a 32 year old construction worker that usually built retail store buildings, and had, in-fact, worked on a store just a block from Danny's apartment. Realizing that, and attempting to narrow down the details, Danny did admit that he had watched that construction crew quite often, since they were usually working shirtless, and a number of the hunkier guys did usually wear cutoffs. Jake admitted that, "Yes, I was probably one of the guys you were watching. I always wear some kind of shorts when the weather is warm enough and I really do like to go shirtless whenever possible."

Looking over toward Jake as he mentioned what he normally did or did not wear on the job, Danny commented, "Well Jake, I will admit, maybe it was that chest and those arms that I looked for whenever I drove past that site. I will admit, you are built like a brick shit house, and I do mean that in a very good way! You're a hot looking man! Nice body!"

"Well, you think I've got a nice looking body now – just you wait until I can drop these shorts and show you the part I'm most proud of!"

Within a minute, Jake and Danny had reached Jake's front door, and as they entered, Jake asked, "Hey, man, want something to drink? I've got some Bud in the frig if you want."

Danny accepted the offer, and with Jake's instruction he did go to the kitchen and retrieved two Buds from the refrigerator as Jake excused himself and went into the bedroom.

Danny was seated at the dining room table, part of the living room area as Jake came back out from the bedroom, fully and completely naked and hot as hell! Danny was shocked beyond belief with the sight that had just walked in. Jake's mid brown highly toned body, all of the muscles in his chest, his arms, his legs and of course his butt were absolutely beautiful and outstanding! His chest tapered down to a waist line that Danny felt like he could simply put his hands around, and the washboard stomach was enough to make any grown man overly jealous of!

"Oh, my God! Oh, shit, man – you look good! Oh, Jake, I sure as hell never expected you to just come out of there all naked and bare like that! Shit man! I thought I'd wrestled some pretty well built guys in the past, but fuck man – nothing that looks like you! Oh, man, you are hot! Oh, my god man – you have got the dick of death on you man, you do! How fucking long is that thing?"

"Well, to be honest, right now not as long as it will be if I can get you to touch it again! It's not hard yet! Come on Danny, touch it and make it get really hard!"

With his mouth hanging open in shock, Danny did slowly, as if maybe he could get an electrical shock, he reached out and touched the top of Jake's rod. It jerked and kind of jumped.

"Yeah, man, yeah! Come on Danny grab ahold of it like you used to do to Todd's dick. Grab me, man, grab me!"

As Danny did slightly grab onto it slightly tighter, he looked up at Jake and said, "Hey, guy, I never got to grab onto Todd's like this. He always had pants or briefs or something on. His was never sticking out all naked like this! Oh, shit, man, you have got one fucking big dick on you."

"So you never got to feel Todd's dick bare then, uh?"

"No, no never did."

"Did you want to Danny? Were you wanting to?"

As Danny slid his hand slightly up the length of Jake's rod, he stood there watching what his hand was doing, and he uttered slightly, "Yeah, yeah, once or twice."

"So you never got to touch his bare dick at all – never?"

"No, no."

"Ever touch any other guy's bare dick?"

Still just standing there and watching Jake's dick get stiffer and stiffer as he moved his hand even more and more, back and forth, Danny finally said, but in a very low tone, "Once. Just once. In the shower, once at school. Mikey Johnson was jerking on his dick and wanting guys to grab it, and so I did and about three other guys did too."

"Oh – so this Mikey Johnson. A gay guy? Was he gay, that why he wanted guys to grab it?"

Now using both hands on Jake's dick since it was getting close to full growth, Danny continued to look at it and answered, "Yeah, I guess he was. But that was at the end of the school year, and he didn't come back to our school the next year. So I just kinda guess he was."

"Did your buddy Todd grab it too?"

"No, no! No if Todd had been there I wouldn't have touched it. Todd wasn't there."

"So tell me Danny. How did it feel to you – that Mikey's dick? Like the feel of it?"

"I guess. I mean, I didn't get sick by touching it or anything like that, but yeah, it was kinda funny. Didn't feel anything like this one though! It was so different!"

"So different? Why was it different? What's different?"

As he continued to stand there close in front of Jake and continued to rub Jake's hard-on he replied, "Don't know! Yours is so much tighter. Yours feels more like a log or a steel pipe. Yours is hot! It feels like it's full of fire inside! Mikey's was too soft, even though he had a hard on."

Was he a white guy or a black guy?"

"Oh, he was white. He felt white."

"He felt white!? What in the hell do you mean by he felt white?"

Looking up at Jake's face, since Jake stood six foot two or three and Danny was more like five feet eleven, he said, "Jake, I've wrestled a lot of black guys, and they all feel tighter, more solid, more like they have muscle all over 'em, and us white guys, we all feel soft and fluffy. I like to feel black men whenever I can, and so look at me now, I'm standing here feeling a black man's dick! Never done that before, but I'm glad I'm getting a chance to do it. I've always wondered what a black man's dick would feel like."

"So – how's it feeling to you? Feel like you expected it to?"

"Yeah, I guess, well maybe better than I really expected. It's so hard! Jake, your dick is really, really hard!"

"Well, I told you that if you touched it, it'd get hard. How's the size of it looking to you now?"

"I can't believe it man, I can't! Jake, I've seen some pictures of some black dicks and man, this is bigger than any I've ever seen in pictures."

"Pictures, uh? Been looking at black dick pictures, uh?"

Then looking up at Jake's face again, Danny admitted, "Yeah, yeah. Yes, I've looked at some gay magazines before! Yeah, man, yeah, I've looked at 'em wondering just what they were like."

"And now here you stand – right?"

"Yeah, right! I will admit that earlier, over in the park – yeah I wanted you to pull it out, I wanted to see it and touch it, but I'm glad you didn't."

"Glad I didn't? Why, if you wanted me to do it? Why you glad I didn't?"

"Cause if you had, then maybe you would not have suggested we come over here. I'm glad we did."

"Well, I'm glad too Danny, but explain something to me."

"Uh, what? What Jake?"

"Why am I the only guy standing around in here in the nude? Come on man, let me see what you've got hidden in there. It's poking out on those Levi's you got on, so I wanna see it and touch it. Come on man – strip man – strip! It's just you and me here. Nobody else is gonna be here. Gonna do it, gonna? Gonna let me see you? I wanna see that hot body of yours man! I wanna see it!"

"But Jake, you told me that if I came over here all was gonna happen was for you to show me you dick. You said that was all."

"Well yeah, yeah I did! But Danny, that was before I found out that you and Todd like to grab each other and before I knew you had been looking at black dicks in some gay mags! Face it man, face it! You know damn well that right now all you'd like to do is strip it all off and finally have some, man to man fun like you've seen in the magazines and have been wanting you and Todd to do! Right? Am I right?"

"Oh, Jake, maybe, maybe! Jake, I've never been with a man like this before. Seriously man, I don't know what I'm supposed to do if I do strip down. I've never done anything like this before."

"And if you don't do it today, then tomorrow and the day after that and the day after that you will still be saying, I've never done this before. Come on man, nothing's gonna happen that you don't want. Ever been sucked off by a guy before? Well – hell I guess not if you've never played with a guy! Ever thought maybe you'd kinda like to feel some guy's mouth on your dick? Ever wanted that?"

"No, of course I've never been sucked off by some guy before – hell not even by some gal, and yes, I've wondered about it. The magazines always say it's so hot to feel that! Jake, is it really that good? I assume you must suck guys off, right?"

"Oh, yeah, man, yeah! Sucking some, man's dick is the glory of the day. And yes, getting your dick sucked feels just as good."

"Jake, do guys suck on your dick? Can guys suck on that big thing?"

"Oh, hell yes man, hell yes! I gotta admit, my dick is the dick of the night whenever I'm out at one of the bars. Guys love big dicks, and since I'm pretty open to letting guys know I've got a big dick, I get a lot of sucking offers. Some of the guys can really do it! They can pretty well deep throat me, and then there are the ones that once they do me, or try to, they never get another chance. Why waste my time with guys that can't suck, when there are plenty of others that are anxious and eager, and I know how far down into the back of their throats I can poke my rod!"

All of a sudden, Danny did realize that all of this type of talk was getting him very excited and wanting to get something going, even though he was not just sure what. He stood there in the living room area and after looking around to make sure all the widows were covered, he completely stripped everything off.

"There! That's it man, not nearly as hot as you, but that's me!"

"Hey, Danny, not bad! You're not really husky, but for a guy your age, you're definitely hot and looking good. And yeah, you've got a dick! Danny, you've got a good dick on you! It's thick man! For a guy your size, you've got a really thick dick! Come over here! Stand here in front of me, I'm gonna give you a taste of getting it sucked, okay? Want that?"

"Oh, Jake, you gonna!? You gonna suck on my dick? Are you!?"

"Hell yes man, hell yes! You want it, don't you?"

"Oh, hell yes man, hell yes! Oh, shit, man I never thought that today, I'd finally be getting my dick sucked! Oh, Jake, yeah, man, yeah! Suck me – let me feel it man – I wanna feel your mouth on it! Oh, man, I can't believe that I'm really gonna stick my dick is some guy's mouth and he's gonna suck on it! And Jake, especially some hot looking guy like you! I think I was always afraid that if I ever did get it sucked off, it'd be by some funny looking wimpy guy, and sure as hell never by some hot looking guy like you! Oh, man, I can't believe this! Yeah, man, yeah, I want you to suck me, man, I do!"

Jake sat down on the edge of the couch, pulled Danny over in position in front of himself, and sucked it in!

Danny stood there for probably three or four minutes letting Jake suck his dick in as far as possible, and then Danny said and asked, "Hey, man! Jake, can I lay down on the floor. My legs are getting weak man, they are."

Jake pulled off of Danny's dick and let him lay down on the floor. Jake then took his position on top of Danny and again sucked all of Danny's dick into his mouth! For probably fifteen or twenty minutes Jake sucked and sucked on Danny's cock to give him the best feeling that he had ever had in his dick. All of a sudden he knew and could tell that Danny was just about ready to give him a mouth full of Danny cum.

"Oh, Jake, Jake, I gotta cum man – I gotta cum!"

Without pulling off, Jake shook his head up and down to let Danny know that he had heard him, and at the same time grabbed onto Danny's hips tighter and tighter letting Danny know that Jake wanted whatever he was about to get. And Jake knew that what that was, was gonna be some good warm soft cum shots, right out of the end of Danny's cock!

With his body going rigid, his arms pushing down on the floor, his hips poking up and his dick firmly placed in Jake's mouth, Danny started yelling, "Oh, oh, oh man, I'm cumming man – I'm cumming! Oh, man! Oh, man – oh that feels so good – oh Jake – oh that feels so good!"

Jake drained all of Danny's cum from the depths of his dick and beyond, and then slowly started licking on Danny's stomach as he laid there and attempted to regain some strength back into his fully drained body. Danny felt whipped and drained. Feeling Jake slowly licking up and down along the middle of his chest and stomach felt good, damn good!

"Oh, Jake, Jake, that feels so good man, that feels so good! Oh, man I never dreamt that having a guy doing stuff to you could feel so good! Oh, man it feels good."

Just then, Jake leaned up from laying on Danny and said, "Hey, guy, turn over. Lay on your stomach for a minute."

Danny had no idea of what and why Jake wanted him to turn over, but in his state of splendor he just did it and did not ask any question.

Just as Danny flipped over, Jake repositioned himself with his legs on the outside of Danny's, and his face right at Danny's ass! Slowly he lowered his face down, softly he blew some nice warm breath at Danny's ass, and with his tongue out, he started licking Danny's ass and the crack in-between the mounds of his tight, little, white ass.

"Oh, man, oh man! Oh, Jake! Oh, man! Oh, man, that feels so good! Oh, my God Jake, oh my God! Oh, Jake, you're licking on my ass aren't you? Oh, man, you're actually licking my ass aren't you man? Oh, man, oh man! Oh, Jake! Oh, Jake, that feels so fucking good! Oh, I've never ever had anybody do that to me! Oh, what a feeling man – what a feeling! Oh, yeah, man, oh yeah! Oh, do it to me, man, do it! Oh, Jake I can feel your face in my ass, oh man, I can feel it!"

Slowly and of course with Danny's very excited encouragement, Jake did continue licking on his butt, but then he took both hands and softly and slowly pulled the crack open and exposed Danny's ass hole! He slid his tongue in!

"Oh, my God man!! Oh, Jake!! Oh, man!! Oh, Jake!! Jake, you're putting your tongue in my ass aren't you!? You're putting your tongue in my ass!!?? Oh, I can't believe it! Oh, man, I can't believe it! Oh, Jake, push it man – push it in! Oh, yeah – oh yeah! Oh, I love that! Oh, I love that! Oh, what a fucking feeling! Oh, what a fucking feeling! Oh, man I can't believe you just put your tongue up in my ass, I can't believe it! Oh, what a great feeling man – I love that! Oh, I love that! Oh, what a feeling! Oh, I just got my ass tongue fucked didn't I? You just fucked my ass with your tongue, didn't you!? Oh, man I wish I could have seen you doing that to me, man, I do! I wish I could have seen that!"

As Jake raised up some and did pull his tongue out of the tight hole, he did utter a, "Yeah, yeah! I did. Guess maybe you kinda liked that, uh?"

"Oh, my God yes I did! Oh, Jake I have never felt anything that felt that fucking good! Oh, shit, man I like that, shit, man, I do! Oh, man I can't believe it man – your face and your tongue and my ass hole! Oh, shit, man, that's hot!"

Slowly Jake maneuvered himself up slightly onto Danny's back and positioned his ragging hard on right up along the crease of Danny's butt. Almost instantly Danny let out with a, "Whoa, whoa! No, no Jake, no! No don't put that in me, man, don't! It's too big man it's too big and I ain't never had anything stuck up in my ass before, please Jake, don't do that!"

"Hey, I'm not Danny, I'm not! I just wanted to let your ass feel it laying there. No, I know you're not ready for that yet. I didn't mean to scare you! I wasn't gonna put it in you, I just wanted to lay here on you and let you and your ass feel it up against you! You okay? I didn't mean to scare you! I didn't."

"I'm okay, I'm okay! I thought there for a minute you were gonna try and put that thing up in me and I know damn well there is no way in hell I'll ever be able to take something like that up in my ass. My ass ain't that fucking big!"

As Jake laid across Danny and slowly licked the back of Danny's neck and the top of Danny's shoulders, he replied, "Oh, yeah, man, yes you will. I know, right now it might be feeling kinda big to you, but give you some time and you're gonna be begging for it, believe me, man, you will!" Trying to turn his head some so that he could kinda look back at Jake, Danny asked, "What do you mean, I will sometime? You sound like we're gonna be doing this again sometime. That what you mean? That what you're saying!?"

"Hell yes man, hell yes! Of course! Admit it man, you like what's going on here, and I sure as hell do too! You got a hot body to play with and to feel! Yeah, we're gonna be doing this a lot! Remember man – your buddy is about to move away, and you're gonna need somebody to be friends with, and I think we could really have some fun together, and do some fun stuff together, now don't you?"

"Man, I guess so, I guess so. Jake, I thought we were just coming over here so you could show me your dick, and now we're really getting into other stuff. I didn't expect this."

"Well? A problem with that? You're having fun, aren't you? You like this don't you?"

"Yeah, yeah, yeah I guess I gotta admit it, I do. Jake, I just never thought about me having sex with some guy though. I just never thought about doing this kind of stuff."

"Hey, Danny, don't tell me you never wanted to play with your buddy Todd, or one of the other guys you've wrestled. You've already told me about grabbing Todd's dick and squeezing it. Face it! Guys don't do that unless he's wanting to do something more with it, right?"

"Well yeah, I guess. Yeah, Jake, I guess with you I can be pretty honest since I'm laying here all naked and you're laying on top of me all naked and you just gave me a blow job, yeah, I admit it, I've wanted to play around with Todd like this for a long time. There was another guy that I wrestled once too, that I really wanted to do something with too. He was a black guy from over at Lake High, and when we wrestled, I swear he got a hard-on and I always wanted to take it out and look at it. I think he had a really big one too! I do! It felt like it, but I couldn't grab it like I wanted to. I was wishing that we could shower together just so I could see it, but of course we didn't get to, since he was from a different school."

"Oh, so maybe that's why you were kinda anxious to see mine then, right? You remember that black guy's dick, and so that's made you kind of interested in mine, right?"

"Well maybe, yeah, maybe so. Jake, I admit, ever since that wrestling match that day, I admit, I've always been kinda interested in seeing some other black man's dick – but I've never gotten to until today."

"Well even now, you haven't really seen it like I think you need to!"

And with that statement, Jake rolled over and off of Danny, and laid on his back, beside him. His rod was stiff and hard, and standing straight up in the air!

"Come on man, play with it! Grab it and jerk it around some. You had your hands on it earlier, but get to it now! Just make believe it's that cock on that black wrestler a few years ago, and play with it and feel it."

Danny did turn over to his side, and as Jake was telling him to grab it, he did reach out and wrap a hand around it, well as far as he could.

"Shit man! Jake, how long is this thing? Jake, how long is this?"

Pointing to the tip and back right at the edge of his bag, Jake replied, "Well, from here to here, I've measured it right at ten and a half inches. So it's not the longest one, since I know some guys have dicks that measure a little more than twelve inches, but hey, I make do with what I have."

"And Jake, you said guys do suck you off? Guys can actually get their mouth on this and down on it far enough to suck you off?"

"Yeah, yeah. Yeah, I will admit, it usually takes a little practice, unless the guy is used to other big dicks, but I've had my number of guys that had never taken a really big dick in their mouth, and after a little practice managed to do it. You'll do the same."

"ME!!?? You think I'm gonna be able to suck this fucking tanker off, you gotta be kidding! Jake, I can't even get my mouth open that far, let alone put that thing in it!"

"Hey, man, every guy I've trained on it has said the same thing. I've never had a newcomer that immediately said, 'Oh, yeah, man, I can suck that thing.' Everyone of 'em were just like you, huffing and puffing just looking at it and touching it, but claiming there was no way in hell they could ever take that much dick in their mouths. You'll learn, believe me, man – you'll learn."

"Hey, Jake, you're still talking like we're gonna be doing this stuff again sometime, and I'm not sure if we are or not."

"Danny, we are! I assure you, we are. I know enough about you already that I know you're gonna be back over here and not too

long from now. You've already told me you and Todd like to jerk and
squeeze each other's cocks, and a minute ago you were telling me
about that black wrestler that you wanted to get to and do something
with, and so now you've got me, the willing partner that wants you
to play with me anyway that you want. Every thought about fucking
some guy in the ass?"

"What!? What? Oh, Jake, no I've never thought about it. You
gotta remember I've never done anything with a guy before tonight!
Why? You wanting me to fuck you? Cause I know man, there is no
way in hell you are gonna get that fucking big thing close to my ass
hole! You about scared the shit out of me earlier when I thought you
were gonna poke me then. No way, you're gonna fuck my ass! You'd
have to take me to a hospital after you tore me all open with it."

"Well, why didn't I have to do that with the other guys that
I've given this dick to? Nothing bad happened to them – well except
maybe for the fact that a couple of 'em have told me that all they want
to get fucked by now is a dick the same size of mine. Believe me,
man, you'll take it, maybe not right now, but you'll take it. I think I
know you well enough already, to know you want it! Hell man – look
at the way you're laying there looking at it and rubbing it. You almost
look like you're in love with it already! Your eyes are just loving it
man, they are!"

"Jake, I gotta admit, I've never seen anything like it before.
I've looked at the pictures in the magazines, and yeah, I've seen some
gay pornos that had big black men fucking some little white guy, but
honestly man, none of 'em had dicks like this one! I can't believe it!
Man, it's so fucking big! And it's so fucking stiff and solid! It's like
a wooden baseball bate!"

"Oh, so now I'm finding out that you've watched some gay
fuck films, right!? Did you and Todd watch those together?"

"No, no! No, Todd doesn't even know I've seen 'em! I
wouldn't tell him that! I saw 'em once when I was in Philly and some
guy had some and he wanted me to watch 'em. He was staying at the
same hotel, and I know damn well he was hoping they'd make me
horny for having sex with him, but he was a real turn off, and besides,
I'd never done anything and I didn't want to do anything with him."

"Was he a black guy or a white guy?"

"Oh, he was white, and I swear, I don't think his skin had ever seen the sun. Pale as a white duck! He turned me off. Especially when he took his shirt off! Man, he was bad! No way man, no way!"

As Danny laid there and handled Jake's rod, Jake just laid back and relaxed, knowing that what was really happening was that – Danny was getting used to it. Just by the look in Danny's eyes, Jake could tell Danny really was wanting it, either in his mouth, or up in his ass, and he really was enjoying it – just having it in his hands! But he also knew he was just gonna have to give Danny time to accept it – on his own time schedule. As Jake laid there watching Danny rub his dick and manage to ever so slightly get his face closer and closer to it, he decided that he was starting to like Danny enough, that he was willing to take whatever time and effort necessary, to get Danny into being a full playmate. He decided he did not want to scare him off! He wanted to fuck that cute little tight white ass that Danny had, and he knew it wasn't gonna happen this night.

"So tell me, man, you gonna fuck my ass for me tonight or not?"

"Oh, Jake, I don't know. Hell man, compared to that dick of yours, mine is small enough that I'm not even sure you'd feel it or not."

"Oh, yeah, man – yes, I'd feel it! Yeah, I've got a big dick, but believe me, man, I don't fuck myself – so I'm happy with any dick some guy has got, and will poke up in my ass hole! Come on man, fuck me – I want you to! Okay? Do it? Come on man, I wanna feel you put that dick of yours up in my ass! I need it! I want it! Come on, do it!"

"Oh, man, my dick is so small compared to yours, I doubt that you'd even feel it!"

"Oh, yeah, man – yeah – I'd feel it! Believe me, man, I'd feel it! Come on man, I wanna feel you fuck me with that dick of yours! Come on, and I know you really do wanna do it – right? You might as well get yourself some anxious hot black ass tonight too! And it's anxious man, it is! I want you to fuck me! Danny, let's do it! I know it's gonna only get hotter and hotter between us from this night on!

You finally got yourself a big black man, with a big black dick! And I know you wanna play with that dick, and not just tonight, so let me see how good your dick fits up inside of me, ok?"

"Oh, Jake, I don't know! Jake, I've never played with some guy like this! I've never fucked some guy's ass man, I never have!

"OK then Danny, just lay on my back and just lay there. Let me roll over here, and you just lay on my back and let your dick poke down between my ass cheeks, and just see what it feels like to lay on a man, all bare and naked."

Jake rolled over so that Danny could just lay himself down on Jake's back and let his cock slide down between Jake's butt cheeks.

"There guy, there! How's that feeling? Feeling good to you?"

"Yeah, oh yeah! Yeah, Jake, I gotta admit, this feels good. Of all my wrestling days, and of all the guys that I have wrestled, this is the first time that I've ever been able to just lay on a man, and feel him up against me. Yeah, Jake, yeah, this feels good. You know, when you are wrestling, you just have to keep moving, and then even if you win the match, you still can't just lay there, on top of the guy and feel him. Yeah, Jake, this is nice! I like this!"

"Hey, Danny, just kind of slide around on me there. Yeah, man, yeah! Move a little back and forth and let our skins slide back and forth against each other! Yeah, man, yeah! Oh, Danny that feels good to me! How's that feeling to you? Feel OK man? Feel OK?"

Laying across Jake full length, letting their bodies slide back and forth and letting each other feel the other man and his skin, Danny answered, "Oh, yeah, man, this is good! Yes, I like this! Have never ever, been able to just lay on top of a man like this before, and besides, hell, I've never even touched a man like you before. Oh, Jake, thank God you are built like the hunk that you are, cause man, if you had not been, I'm sure I would have just run for the door when you came out here all bare and naked and showing everything! I will admit, that was one fucking hot sight to see something like you come walking around the corner looking like that! Jake, you are one fucking hot stud man, you are!"

"Hey, Danny, thanks! Thanks man, thanks! Now, I gotta tell you that your 'fucking hot stud' that you are laying on top of, he really does need his ass fucked. Danny, the whole time you been laying up there I could feel that rod of yours getting stiffer and stiffer down there between my butt bubbles, and I know damn well it wants to go find a nice little home up in my ass!"

"Danny, grab that tube of lube laying there, and squirt some up in my hole, and stick your dick up in there, I need to feel you poking my hole!"

This time without any complaint, Danny did as Jake asked. He pulled his hands out from under Jake's armpits, where he had been firmly grabbing onto as he slid back and forth on Jake's body, he reached over, grabbed the lube, moved himself slightly out of the way, shot a quick shot of lube into Jake's hole, and then grabbed his own hard-on and without so much as a word, poked Jake's hole full.

"Oh, my God yes, oh yes!" Jake excitedly let out, with a definite smile in his voice! "Oh, Danny, do it man, do it! Danny you are now fucking a great big black construction worker, one of the guys that you used to look at up on the building, and you are now fucking him good! Do me, man – fuck me – fuck me hard! Danny feed me, man, feed me! Fuck it hard man, fuck it hard! Never thought you'd get to fuck one of those construction workers did you? Never thought you'd be in one of their asses did you man?"

"Oh, fucking shit no man, no I didn't! Jake, man, oh man, your ass is fucking hot man, fucking hot! Oh, shit, man, I never knew a big muscled ass could feel this fucking good! Oh, Jake, I can't believe I almost did not do this tonight! Oh, shit, man, what a fucking turn on! Oh, Jake, thank God I did it man!! Oh, thank God I did it! Oh, Jake – how in the hell do you know how to get guys to do stuff that they say they aren't gonna do? Oh, shit, man, I can not believe this! Oh, man – oh man – oh Jake – I'm gonna cum man, I'm gonna! I gotta man, I gotta! Oh, shit here it comes man – here it comes! I'm cumin man – I'm cummmmmmm! Oh, shit! Oh, man alive, wow! Oh, Jake – I just shot everything I had man – I did! Jake, I shot everything! Oh, crap man, I am beat! Shit man, I'm exhausted! Fucking exhausted!"

Danny totally collapsed down on Jake, and took deep, deep breaths just trying to re-coop some.

"Danny my man! Danny, I gotta tell you that I have not been fucked like that in one hell of along time! Seriously man, even Ralphie, my construction buddy that fucks me more than anybody else, does not fuck me that good! Danny, you know how in the hell to fuck a butt man, you do! Danny, Ralphie is another black guy, built just about like me, hung just about like me, but let me tell you, he sure as hell does not fuck like you do! If you really have never fucked around with any guys before, this is gonna be a life changing day for the gay community around this town! Shit man, your days of saying you don't fuck with guys, are over!"

"Oh, Jake, you serious man, you serious?"

"What about guy, what about?"

"You said I fuck better than your buddy Ralphie does! You serious? You serious, or are you joking?"

"Serious as hell man, serious as hell! He might be big, and have a tank for a dick, but he sure as hell does not know how to use it like you do yours! You are one hell of a good fucker! Man, you know what you are doing! Now, all we gotta do is talk you into letting me use my little dickie on that ass of yours! When we gonna do that?"

"Jake, I don't know, I don't know! But, I will tell you one thing! You sure as hell have got the talent in getting somebody to do things that they say they are not gonna do – like reaching over and feeling your dick in a public park – like coming over here – like getting me to take all my clothes off – like touching your dick and jerking on it – like letting you suck on me, and yeah, man, yeah – like getting me to fuck you! Jake, I do not know when we're gonna do that, but the way you manage to get me to do stuff that I thought I'd never be doing – hell man – probably the very next time we get together! I'm not very good at convincing you that I'm not gonna do stuff, and just like all the other stuff – now that I have a new friend, I'm sure it will be the next time! Whenever I can come back and let you talk me into doing some more stuff, that I swore I'd never ever do!"

"Danny my boy, I love what you're saying, I do! You just told me that you are gonna be coming back, and I'm just telling you that when you do, you are gonna find out just up real close, just what my dick can do for that ass of yours, and you are gonna find out too, that you can suck on a much larger fudge-sickle than you ever thought! Danny, sorry about your bad day, but look how it's all turning out for you! You and me! You got more than just a friend man, you got one hell of a lot more! You sure didn't expect that earlier tonight, did you?"

STRAIGHT, MARRIED, AND IN BROWN PARK

"Hey, guys, let's go use that back booth. OK?"

Shawn, Gary and Wes had pre-planned to meet at their local gay bar, 'The-Boys-Will-Be-Boys-Bar,' and were looking for a very private space to have a very private conversation. The three men each got a beer from the bartender and headed for the back of the bar, to the most private spot. They wanted to have some conversation that others could not overhear.

"OK guys." Shawn said after they got situated in the booth. "OK, did you guys find out anything yet?"

"Yeah, we think we did." Wes replied. "Gary thinks he found what we are looking for, and we just need until after Thursday evening to confirm it."

As Shawn looked across the table at Gary and Wes, he then asked. "OK Gary, what did you find? Fill me in guys!"

"Shawn, there is this guy that works out at the same gym that I use. His name is Jon. I found out that he is married, heard him talking about his 19th anniversary coming up next week and about his boy and girl planning on throwing them an anniversary party. He looks like he is about maybe 41 or 42, and I know he is six foot one, and weighs in at 195. When he did his monthly weigh in at the gym, I just happened to be there, and after seeing his weight, I then asked him how tall he was and he told me six foot one. Good body! Damn good body! He works for some kind of a design firm. So he's a white shirt type of guy, but a damn well built one! He's got a hot body that he has really worked on! I've asked around some, and I know that he is at the gym twice a week, Monday and Fridays, and he – now catch this – he runs three times a week! That's our ace in the hole! He runs about two miles on Tuesday, Wednesday and Thursday evenings. That's why we need till at least Friday before we are ready to make a move. I want to make sure, for his next two run days, that he always runs the same course. He runs over at Brown Park, and Shawn, you know how many hiding places are in that place. A little after dark, hell, you could live in there and nobody would know it. And, come to think of it, I'll bet a bunch of homeless guys do!"

"Great! Sounding great so far guys!" Shawn exclaimed. "So do you know anything about his attitudes or have any feelings about if he could handle this or not?"

"Yeah – I kind of think I do – maybe a little." Gary replied. "In the locker room a couple of times I've heard guys make negative comments about the gays in town and he never jumps in and agrees with them when they are getting nasty. He doesn't seem to really appreciate that type of talk. One day when I could hear some of them in the next locker row over, they were talking that way, and this Jon guy was getting dressed in my row, and to see what he would do, I grabbed my crotch as if to offer it to him, and he laughed and just said – 'Sorry, I'm a married straight guy!' I was kind of just acting like I was playing back to the shit, that those other guys were spilling out, but at least I got a chance to kind of make a slight offer to him. He did not get mad, but then he didn't come over and grab it either! Oh – yeah – an added plus to the picture – hung like a damn horse! I haven't seen it hard yet, but shit – that day I was ready to find out right there, what his attitude was!"

Then looking at Wes, he continued. "Well, not like you and yours – but hey, a big dick that I was ready for anyway!"

"So you really have no idea if he has ever done anything or not then, right?" Shawn asked.

"No, I really don't know for sure. I don't have any way of really knowing!" Gary replied. "But I do know he is a married, straight, guy!"

"Gary, do you think that if we put this off for one more week, that you can manage to get some kind of a conversation going at the gym and try to find out if he has ever done a guy before or not? I really want to see if we can find us a guy that has never been with a guy before. Think you can work that out?"

"Well, hell Shawn, I sure can try. You know, the locker room conversations are pretty open once in awhile. If I set out to see what I can do, then maybe I can get it done. So you want to put it off one more week and let me see what I can find out?"

"Yeah, Gary! Let's do! I really do want a virgin guy if at all possible!" Shawn replied.

"Well Shawn. If I find out this guy has been with other guys, do you want to just drop him and move on to somebody else or what?" Gary asked.

"No, I wouldn't say to just drop him. I like the physical description that you gave for him, and regardless of, even if he has been with a guy, I want him too. But if he is a gay virgin, wow – how much better! And if he is virgin, and we already know that, it just makes everything that much more fun, since we really know what we have at hand! But you do know for sure that he is a married straight guy, right? And he's a daddy, too?"

"Yeah, I know for sure he is a married straight guy, and he has two kids. A boy and a girl. Yeah, he's the married kind of a guy! Now we just need to hope he's the married, straight, daddy type of a guy that might like to do something a little different for a change. Maybe get some spice in his life for a change!" Gary added.

"Shaw?" Wes asked. "What we're doing – couldn't this be called rape if we got caught? I mean, doing this against someone's will, isn't that getting pretty dangerous?"

"Hey, Wes, I'd rather call it, "Giving a guy a new perspective!"" That's why we find out just as much about the guy as possible – so that he understands that if he makes any trouble, then we could expose him as the one that got it started. When he finds out we know who he is, and a lot of personal stuff about him, then he is much more willing to walk away. But! Hey, don't worry about it. When I used to do this up in Minneapolis, practically every one of them wanted to know how to stay in contact so they could do it again. Let's face it – it really does give them a new perspective. That's why I really do like to find the married daddies that have never done it with a guy! They are the ones that can really get all carried away with it. Scares the shit out of them at first, too! They think they are going to be all physically altered for the rest of their lives, but then pretty soon they find out they really are OK. At first they think it is wrong, but then they pretty quickly change their minds. I've only had one guy that really got all pissed about it, and hell, he was some religious fanatic anyway. He was the kind of a guy that if you gave somebody some money to go get something to eat on, he would have a problem of some kind! Probably something like – make him go get a job, and learn how to feed himself! You know guys, actually most of the, so-called, straight guys out there want to have gay sex, but they just need someone to force them into it the first time. They don't have the guts to tell another guy he wants to either suck that guy or get sucked by that guy, so he doesn't do anything at all, until – until some other guy forces it on him. Then he's actually glad, and he has finally had his first time! He's had his first good time with some other guy!"

Shaw was 24, five foot-eleven, 180 pounds, muscular well built body, light brown hair and a completely bare chest. Nice seven inch dick that did have the ability to get very stiff and rigid when appropriate.

Gary was also 24, stood right at five feet-nine, 165 pounds, and although a good body, not as muscular as Shawn's. Sandy colored hair with a nice trail that went right down the chest to the bush – in the crotch area. Nice little trail of sandy hair that all of Gary's playmates loved to lick on and bite with their teeth.

Wes was younger. Wes was only 20, or as he would proudly announce: "I will be 21 in just a few weeks." Much smaller guy! Five feet-six, 160 pounds, but about ten of those pounds were all in his dick. Soft – measured a good four and a half inches just hanging, and excited and hard, one very rigid nine and a half inches, of true measurement! And it had been measured by many of a guy, that just would not believe what other guys were trying to tell him. Poor little, young, Wes has been led to the restroom many of times, had his dick jerked on to get it as hard as he could get it, then measured to prove the truth of the 9 and 1/2 inches that were claimed. His friend would then collect the five or ten dollar bet that was on the table, depending on if it was really that big, on 'that little guy, or not.' Wes always managed to corporate nicely and managed to get it as hard as possible, for measuring! He was the money maker for the group, and he did his duty!

Occasionally the bet included another five or ten dollars for being able to prove, or disprove the claim that Wes's hard-on dick also measured at least seven inches around it, when it was good and hard. $20.00 total had often been paid to Wes and his friends when some asshole, simply could not believe that, "some little guy like that," – as he was often referred to – could be hanging that much meat between his legs. Actually it was not a true betting situation. It was much more of a one-sided bet! If they proved what they were saying, then the payment was made. If they were wrong – which just never happened – then it would be just an apology for making an untrue statement. That was always the agreement. Wes and his friends never had any concern about, not collecting the money!

Many of a times, when in, The-Boys-Will-Be-Boys-Bar, all of a sudden some friend of Wes's would come up to him wherever he was at, and simply say, "Hey, Wes. Sorry to bother you, but we need to take this guy to the back room for a moment."

This never created a problem for Wes. He was always very accommodating, since he never wanted to miss a chance of letting some additional man see, and feel his sausage stick. The only problem might be the trying to explain, to somebody that he might be drinking with, of just why he needed to accompany the other guys to the restroom.

Legal drinking age in the state is 21. Wes is in the bar drinking! Seems this should be a problem, right? Wrong! The owner of the bar was one of Wes's regular bottom "boys," although about 35 years older, and with the promise that Wes would not use it anyplace else, he had provided Wes with a good fake ID to have – just in case – the police came into the The-Boys-Will-Be-Boys-Bar. Wes had to promise that he would never attempt to use it at any time, or for any reason, other then to have it at that bar, for 'a just in case,' situation. The owner's rules were: Do as I ask, and you get to drink at The-Boys-Will-Be-Boys-Bar, but if you screw it up at anytime, or if I hear you are using it someplace else, then I will take it back, and you do not get to drink here until you are actually 21. So if you use it like you are told, you can drink, and I will not have a problem of you and your friends doing the betting think in the bar – as long as you do fuck me at least once a week!

The agreement has been in force for more than three years now, and Wes found this arrangement to be very acceptable! In addition, Wes had stood very true to the part of the agreement of, 'at least – once a week!' This had been a blessed agreement, cast down from the heavens, for both Wes and Harry, the bar owner. Wes has now been able to drink in the bar since he was aged eighteen, could get his dick measured and played around with by anybody that wished, and Harry got fucked by this young kid – the one with the telephone pole dick – at lease once a week, and for about the past three years now! And the 'at least' was just that! Wes would often ask for some type of a personal favor, like – oh, perhaps letting some under aged trick of his get a drink, or asking Harry if he could drink naked for a couple of hours late at night, or actually do a jack-off demo right out in the bar when a bunch of guys were all begging for it.

Wes actually begged with Harry one time to let him actually screw some guy right in the bar, if he pledged an extra five fucking sessions for him over the next two weeks. The "bottom" was really getting obnoxious with everybody, and was bragging about just how easily, and how quickly he could, and would be able to take Wes's dick – if – he ever had the chance. The crowd considered the man nothing but hot air! The entire bar crowd wanted to see Wes ram his pole up in that guy and shut him up once and for all. Everybody was convinced that the big mouth would scream for mercy, and they wanted to be there when it happened.

It happened! Wes screwed him, right in the bar! Harry got the promise of five extra screws over the next two weeks, and the big mouth did scream for mercy, just before he jumped up from the floor, grabbed his pants and headed out the door, running! The bar crowd got to see it all happen!

The last thing the crowd heard from the obnoxious guy, as he was running out the side door, was, "Oh, God! Oh, God damn that hurt! Oh, Shit man! Damn, my ass hole is ripped!"

Harry knew that letting these things happen in his bar was very risky, and was putting his liquor license on the line, but knowing that if he allowed it, meant that later that night, he was going to be feeling Wes's ten inches long and seven inches around, up in his ass, and that made him a very agreeable person.

The three men finished their beers and agreed that Gary would see what additional information he could uncover about Jon, and that he would verify that Jon did use the same running route each time he ran. They decided to re-meet Sunday night at 8 PM here at the bar, and at that time they would make additional plans or alter those that they were currently working with.

As the men were ready to leave the bar, Gary and Shawn decided that they wanted to stop by the Crotch Bar and have another drink. Since Wes was not, of quite yet, legal age to be in another bar, he decided to hang around The-Boys-Will-Be-Boys-Bar, and see if Harry was going to happen in a little later. Wes knew that regardless of how empty his plate might be on any given night, anytime he wanted some ass and some good strong sucking, all he needed to do was to hang around until Harry showed up.

For Wes, it usually meant, as it did for this night, a couple of beers, quite a number of interesting conversations – usually about size, and of course the normal, almost required trip to the "measuring room," and Harry showed up. Wes heard someone in the back of the bar say, "Harry's here. Wes is smiling!" And then he heard another voice chime in, "Yeah, Wes is happy and smiling, and Wes is going to get it!"

The original voice then added, "Well maybe Wes is going to get it, but Harry is going to be getting it too! And in a big, big way!"

The comments made in the bar did not bother Wes at all. He loved being the center of attention. He loved the fact that all of the guys always wanted to have a piece of his action!

Eight o'clock Sunday evening came, and the three men again met at the back booth.

"OK guys!" Shawn said. "Just where do we stand with this Jon guy?"

"Hey!" Gary responded. "Wes and I followed him both Wednesday and Thursday nights, and he used exactly the same route running as he had last week and this past Tuesday. I'm sure now he uses the same route all the time, and he stops in that north side restroom, takes a piss and rinses his face off every time he does that run. By using that same route, I think he can time himself that way. I worked out at the gym at the same time that he did Friday night. I managed to get some short conversation going while in the locker room, and especially while in the steam room. That was the most successful one. Actually managed to get him to tell me he never has played before. Of course to get him to tell me, I had to really come out of the closet and actually proposition him! Thank goodness he and I were the only ones in the steam room for a few minutes. I really played up to him, and I told him how well built he was, and then I looked at his big dick hanging down, and then I made a mention about it, and then I just told him, well – 'I guess you probably already know I'm a gay guy, don't you?' And then I asked him if I had any chance with him."

"He told me that he certainly did appreciate me making the good comments about him, but he was a married straight guy, and he does not play with guys. He said it really nicely. He did not seem pissed off that I actually had told him that I wanted him. God man! If I am going to be doing this kind of stuff, it sure is good that I don't mind telling guys that I am gay. I managed to get him to tell me he does not play around and if I had been afraid to admit that I was a gay guy, I'm not sure how I could have found out about him. I still think he is not real opposed to the idea though, well anyway he doesn't get nasty when it's talked about."

"After I asked him if I had any chance, he did not get up and move away from me. Our legs were almost, well once actually did, touch, and it did not seem to bother him. When he told me he was a married straight guy, I joking asked, 'Well, that sure don't need to stop you, does it?' He kind of laughed and slightly said, 'Well, guess you could be right, couldn't you?' I still think he is approachable, I really do!"

"Well men!" Shawn then said. "We will find out on Tuesday! We will find out! You two are still in this with me, right? I mean, neither one of you are getting bugged by the idea of doing this are you?"

"Shawn!" Wes said. "Shawn, if I can throw some guy down here on the floor, here in the bar, and fuck the hell out of his little pale ass, while everybody cheers me on, you don't think I'm the kind of a guy that will back out when the hot gets hotter, do you?"

"Hell no Wes!" Shawn answered. "Of all the guys around here, you are the one that I have the most faith in that would run from the east side of town to the west side of town, completely naked and with a ragging hard-on, if you thought it would be fun, sexy, and exciting! You, hell man – you, I would never figure as a quitter! Gary, how about you?"

"Oh, shit, man! I'm in! Hell, I have not been scouting this Jon guy out as long as I have been, just to find out he is a married, straight, guy, and then walk away. Hell no! I'm in! A married straight guy! Shit man! I've never set out to do one like him, as a set goal before. Maybe I have, but just never knew it – since they don't always tell you everything about themselves! Hell, wonder how many married, straight, guys I have played with, and just never knew it? I'll bet it's been quite a number, though."

It's now Tuesday evening – 5:15 PM – at the men's room – North Lakeside Lane in Brown Park, and Shawn, Wes and Gary have gathered.

"OK guys." Shawn said. "As soon as he goes into the restroom, all of us get ready to go in and surround him."

"Hey, Shawn, what do we do if there are other guys in there too?" Wes inquired.

"Let's face it men. We've already been out here for about half an hour ourselves, and there had not been one guy come down this lane yet. Hell man! This place is so deserted I wonder if maybe this Jon guy isn't using it as his running place just in the hope of something funny happening back in here. I kind of wish I had known about this place earlier! It's so out of the way, it's a good place to use, for having some fun."

As the three men were tucked out of sight among the bushes, they saw Jon approaching along the trail. Jon entered the men's room, used the urinal, turned to rinse his face off at the lavatory when Shawn approached him and said. "Hi! I understand you are Jon!"

Jon looked at him in quite a surprised manner and answered. "Yeah. Yeah, I am. How are you? And how do you know me?"

As Shawn moved closer and closer to Jon, he replied. "Oh, hey man. There are a number of us guys here around town that happen to know you and are real anxious to get to know you even better."

Then turning toward the door, he continued. "Hey, Gary and Wes. Jon is waiting for us. He's getting really anxious for us to get started in here, guys."

Gary and Wes came into the restroom and as they did, they said, "Hi."

Jon looked at the two new members of the group and said. "Gary, I know you! You work out at the gym. Gary, what in the hell is going on here? Gary, I don't understand! What is going on?"

Gary walked over to Jon and said. "Well Jon, my man! Remember how I asked you the other day if I had any chances with you? Well, I didn't really get the kind of an answer that I was hoping for, so we kind of set this up so that you can have another opportunity to give me a different answer. My buddies and I are all anxious for you to give us, and our dicks, a good old fashioned blow job."

"Gary! Gary, I don't give guys blow jobs! Gary, I'm not gay. Gary, I'm a straight married daddy! Gary I told you that at the gym the other day!"

"Yeah, yeah we know Jon. That's the excitement of doing this! We really like to give the straight married daddies a chance to do something different than they get to do while with their little ole women. See Jon, we have dicks, and of course you already know, your wife does not have one for you to play with, so here we are! We are all ready and anxious for you to use us, use our dicks and get some real good gay sex!"

As Gary was talking and trying to explain the situation to Jon, Wes and Shawn were stripping their clothes off, and were now standing there completely naked.

Jon looked back and saw that the other two men were naked. He looked at Shawn, and did a very fast double take when he saw Wes's man meat.

"That one is pretty scary isn't it?" Gary asked. "Just imagine, you will get to swallow as much of that as possible in just a few minutes!"

"Gary, please! Gary, I don't know where you got the idea that I want to suck on some guy's cock, but I don't! Gary, I'm straight! Gary, please, let's just get out of here and forget we ever had this conversation in here. Gary, I do not intend to suck on that guy's cock or any guy's cock. Do you understand me? Gary, I'm not sucking any cock!"

As Gary started to remove his shirt and shorts, he then told Shawn and Wes. "Hey, men. Jon is not acting real anxious to work with us on this, so I think maybe the ankle restrains just might be an advantage. Strip those shorts off of him so that he doesn't get any of our cum on them, and then have to go home and explain to the little old wife, of just where that all came from."

Without any warning, as they stripped his running shorts and his jock strap off of him, Jon realized that each men had ahold of an ankle and he was immediately ankle strapped. It had happened so fast, that he had no chance to even attempt to run or try to get out of the restroom. He was not capable of anything more than a very, very short step. Running or even walking normally was now completely out of the question. He was now completely at their mercy!

Shawn and Wes took ahold of Jon's arms and Shawn said. "Hey, man! This is going to be fun! We have ourselves one nice hot looking married, straight, daddy guy, and he is going to take care of us like an old pro. Aren't you, Jon?"

Jon protested and again tried in vain to tell the three that he did not suck cock, and that he was a married guy. He tried to tell them that married guys do not suck off other guys, and they don't get sucked off by guys.

"Yeah, we know!" Replied Wes. "That's why we like you so much. Married guys that have to learn, are the best cock suckers around, and that is why we chose you! Down – get down on your knees, big man – so that you are right at the same level as these cocks, that you are gonna be taking care of!"

Shawn and Wes pushed Jon down on the shoulders. Jon knew what they wanted. They indicated without saying anything that he would do as they wanted. Jon knelt down on his knees. He could not run, and Shawn and Wes both had ahold of his wrists. He was now under their control, and he was only one against three rather healthy young men, that had ideas of their own. He knew that unless something very unexpectedly happened, that he was going to be forced to suck on their cocks, and he had been telling them that he did not want to do that. He kept trying to tell them that married guys do not do this kind of thing.

Jon did not say anything, but his three captors did see him look around to see if there was anything in there, that he could find, that could help him get out of this predicament. He knew the north lakeside lane was very seldom used, and even those that did use it as a running path seldom stopped in the restroom. He told his captors that he seriously was wondering just why in the hell he had stopped in here. He knew he had been doing that as a standard thing, but he now had serious questions as to why he ever started doing – what he had now decided was a very stupid and foolish thing. He told his three men, that he felt very trapped, and he decided that had been the plan of his three captors. He admitted that they were using a very hidden part of the park, and that they had found a very private place to capture somebody and play with somebody, with nobody else close by. He told them that it sure did look like they knew what they were doing!

Once again Jon pleaded. "Hey, guys! Hey, you guys know I don't know how to suck cock and I'm afraid that if I do, I might get sick since I just don't do that! So can I ask you guys again to just let me go, and I will not let anybody know this happened. I'll not say anything to anybody! OK?"

"No – not OK!" Replied Shawn. "No man! We are not going to hurt you any, and I'm sure that by the time we all get done in here you are going to be glad we fed you some dick, but hey man, you are one hot looking, married, straight, guy, and that means you are just the kind of a guy we like to play with. And, oh hey, Jon! Just in case you might just happen to think that you could cause trouble for us after we are all done here, and if we have to talk to the law, we will just blame this all on you and let the papers report how you, the married daddy of two children, one very nice and polite boy, and one very pretty young lady, and one of our city's better design detailer citizens was the instigator of all of these actions and he was the one that made us three have sex with him. We just know too much about you for you to even think about trying to get any revenge, so drop that idea right away! And besides Jon. By the time we are done, I am sure you will be asking how you can get back together with us again so that you can do this all over again, and do us – all again! So see man. It's all going to work out to everybody's advantage. You just don't realize that yet!"

"Come on Jon." Gary said as he walked up close to Jon's face. Gary took his dick in hand, and rubbed it up against Jon's face. Jon held his mouth tightly closed. He shook his head, "No." He indicated that he did not want Gary's cock stuck in his mouth!

"Come on man!" Gary encouraged. "Come on Jon. You might as well take it now, nice and agreeably or we will have to force your mouth open and push it in there. Jon there are three of us here and we all want our cocks sucked on by you, the married straight guy, so you might as well start cooperating or things could get rough for you. Now, are you going to open up so I can use your mouth for some dick fun, or not?"

Gary once again placed the tip of his rod right at Jon's mouth.

Gary placed his hand under Jon's chin, and said, "Come on man. You might as well accept the fact that today you are going to learn how to suck cock, and mine is the first one, so let's get it going man!"

Gary pulled his cock to the side, and slapped Jon's face with it. He repeated that action from the left side.

"OK guys!" Gary said. "Guys he is not cooperating, so I guess it is time to let him know we do mean business. Shawn, how tightly can you grab a bag of balls?"

"Oh, Gary! Oh, Gary I can grab mighty tightly! I'm sure our Jon will know he has been grabbed when I am done."

"OK men, lets see if he is interested in doing me now. Shawn, if he refuses again, you know what to do."

Shawn watched as Gary once again put his dick in front of Jon's face. Shawn saw Jon close his mouth. Shawn grabbed ahold of Jon's bag of balls and started to squeeze. Jon did not open his mouth, so Shawn squeezed a little tighter. Again Jon did not cooperate so Shawn squeezed even more.

Shawn told Gary, "OK Gary. This guy is taking some convincing that we are going to be using him for our enjoyment, so just keep your dick up there good and close and pretty soon he will decide that letting you fuck his face is really better than having his balls all in a whole bunch of little pieces when he goes home! So let's just continue to work with him and pretty soon, he'll start to understand."

"Won't you big man?" Shawn asked Jon.

As Shawn spoke to Jon, he once again tightened up his grip on Jon's balls. Jon let out a groan of pain.

"Ah ha!" Shawn replied with. "So now we are finally finding out just what type of pressure it takes down here to get some actions out of our man, aren't we?"

Shawn squeezed again. Again Jon let out a slight squeal. Shawn squeezed tighter, and jerked on the bag. Jon finally opened his mouth, but, in a futile attempt to once again try to tell his captors that he does not suck cock.

Gary took immediate action as he saw Jon's mouth just slightly start to open. He immediately placed the tip of his cock into Jon's mouth. Jon could not speak.

"Jon!" Gary said. "Jon if you so much as even act like you are going to bite my dick, so help me, man, I will tell Shawn to pull those damned balls right off of you, so don't even think about trying that! I've seen guys that thought they had control, and after Shawn came damn near of – de-balling them – they had a whole new attitude of just what they were willing to do! So believe me, man, his hands are on your balls for a damn good reason, and right now it is to protect my dick!"

With that very specific statement and threat given to him, Jon decided that regardless of how terrible this whole thing was to him, and how totally disgusting it was to even think about putting another man's dick in his mouth – if he wanted to protect the family jewels, he had better cooperate. He relaxed his mouth and let Gary slide some more of his dick in.

"Nice man!" Gary proclaimed. "Shawn, I think we finally got to the man! My dick is about half way in his nice cherry mouth! He finally decided that he likes having his balls down there – didn't you Jon?"

Jon kind of muttered a slight, but not a real convincing, "Yeah." He was letting the three know that he was not at all happy with the idea that he had some guy's dick stuck in his mouth!

As Gary took ahold of Jon's head to have a good and solid control of it for his soon to happen fucking session, he told Shawn. "I think you can let up on the balls some now. My friend up here now seems to realize that getting it down the throat is better than losing his manhood back there, so just stand by an let's see if he is going to be a little better boy, and let me do him the way I like. If he starts giving me any more trouble, then we will go back to using your vice grip hands on his bag!"

Shawn let loose of Jon's bag. Jon actually expressed a little appreciation and attempted to say, or at least mutter, "Thanks."

Gary pushed the rest of his dick into Jon's mouth. He pulled Jon's head completely into his gut, so that he could push his dick back into Jon's throat as far as possible.

Jon choked. He attempted to push off of Gary's dick so that he could cough, and rather gag. Gary pulled his dick back partly, but did not completely remove it from Jon's mouth.

"Jon, my man." Gary asked of his bottom toy. "You OK? You will get used to it pretty soon! Right now you need to be glad it's just my dick you are learning on. Look at that damn big pole of Wes's over there that is just waiting to get his chance at you. Imagine what in the hell your mouth would feel like if it was that damn big pole stuck in there."

As Gary made that statement, Jon did attempt to look somewhat sideways and look at Wes's dick. He had not yet seen it at full staff, and when he did, he uttered and muttered something to the sort of, "Oh, God!"

"One hell of a lot of dick on that little guy, isn't there Jon? That's why I and Shawn are teaching you before you get the real thing. You get the little sticks first, then after we are kind of done with you, then we pass you on to the dick of the day, and let him show you just what sucking on a real stick of meat is all about!"

Jon attempted to say something, but the best that the three tops could figure out was that he was trying to say he could never do that one.

Shawn then told Jon, "Don't worry about that one right now man! You have Gary's and mine to accomplish first before you have to open every tube in your upper body in an attempt to get that one down in there! We won't force that one on you until we know you are ready and can handle it! How is he doing on you, Gary?"

"Well, for a guy that really did try and fight this whole thing as much as he did, I think he is doing pretty good. I can tell he is not really doing any sucking and any actions on his own, quite yet, but he's letting me push my little dick rod in and out of his mouth without too much fighting back. I kind of think maybe he has now found out that having a guy's dick stuck in his throat is not going to make him throw up any, and maybe, just maybe he is now starting to understand that there is more than one way to get a real joy out of that dick of his!"

Gary grabbed ahold of Jon's head and started using it as a piece of jack off equipment.

Jon tried to object and tried to tell Gary to stop, but that only encouraged Gary to continue it and to pick up the speed of action in his mouth.

"Jon, my man!" Gary exclaimed. "You are now getting your face fucked! Shut the hell up, and let me fuck you! This is only the first face fucking that you will be getting today, and right now it is with the smallest cock here, so just shut the hell up and learn how to take a good active face fucking!"

Jon tried to express that this was not good, but he had no control over the actions, so he was forced into cooperating. Gary used Jon's head to his "fucking" advantage. He jerked Jon's head back and forth at his will. Once in awhile, he would grab Jon by the back of his head and just for a moment, he would pull him completely up against his gut and hug his head up against him. Then he would immediately resume his face fucking.

As Gary was taking care of Jon's mouth, or perhaps it was now Jon's mouth taking care of Gary, Wes and Shawn were getting each other all excited by playing around as if they were very young guys, and had never touched another guy before. Slight grabbing and slapping. Just being silly.

As Gary continued his face fucking, he calmly told Jon, "Jon, I'm sure you have never tasted another man's cum before, since this is the first time you've had a cock in your mouth, but today is going to be your introduction to guy cum. I'm starting to get all kind of filled up, and I can tell that it is not going to be too long before I will need to just let it fly, so when you feel something nice and warm hit the back of your throat, you will know you have just been indoctrinated into the real world of cum eaters!"

Jon tried to strongly object and tried to push Gary off of his dick.

"No, no, man!" Gary responded. "No, no! No – don't you try to get off of my dick now man! You've been doing real good here since I finally got it all the way in you, so don't screw things up now. I am going to cum, and you are my boy of choice to take it, and so don't get yourself all excited about it. It's been done millions and millions of times by guys, and even by the gals, and today is just your first time, so get ready. Our talking about me unloading in your throat is getting me all that much more excited, so it is going to fly faster and probably harder now than before."

Gary had resumed his active, fast, rough, and hard fucking of Jon's virgin face. He grabbed ahold of Jon's head firmly since he knew Jon was not anxious or even willing to take a mouth full of cum.

"Oh, Jon! Oh, Jon! I'm cumin! I'm cummmmin!" Gary just almost screamed. Oh, man! You're gonna be eating my cum! It's cummmmin – ohhhhh man – ohhhh man, eat it! Eat it man! Eat it! Eat it! Eat it! Yeah, eat it!!"

Gary had very seriously let it fly! His moaning and groaning was not an act. He had let a very serious cum load hit Jon squarely and fully.

Jon jerked his head back. He pulled off of Gary's stiff, cum dripping dick. He gagged and bent over.

"Swallow man!" Gary barked. "Swallow it! It's OK! Swallow it! Jon, it's better to just let yourself swallow it!"

Jon bent his head over and then attempted to swallow Gary's cum. Part of the mouth full of cum spilled out of Jon's mouth. Gary reached over, grabbed a paper towel from the dispenser and handed it to Jon. Jon wiped his mouth, and then shook his head.

"Hey, guys, can I rinse my mouth out? Can I get some water?" Jon pleaded with his captors.

"Yeah, here I'll help you up." Gary responded.

Gary helped Jon to his feet and over to the lavatory.

"If you think eating my cum is so bad and so sickening, when you put your face close to that lavatory, if you don't throw up from seeing how pathetically disgusting it is, then I don't feel so bad about filling your little virgin mouth so full of man cum."

As Jon rinsed his mouth out, Shawn then took him by the arm and instructed, "OK man! You've done one! Man number two is now real horny after watching you take a mouth full, so back on your knees and open your mouth. I'm the last practice run you get before you have to take Wes's telephone pole, so let's practice and get it good!"

Shawn helped Jon back onto his knees and immediately aimed for Jon's mouth.

"Open up man! I've got myself a hot dick here that wants some of that action that I just saw. I've got a hot load of cum that's been building up for about the past four or five days, and I know just where I want to shoot it! Open up! I want your face!"

Jon looked up at Shawn and pleaded.

"Shawn! I've already been fucked in the face once man! Shawn I'm not used to this kind of stuff man! Please, can you maybe just jerk off or something? Shawn, really man!"

"Jon shut the hell up and open your mouth! I am going to fuck you like Gary got to fuck you, so shut the hell up and open up!"

Jon realized that there was no hope in trying to get Shawn to change his mind about fucking his face. Jon opened his mouth and let Shawn push his dick in.

Shawn grabbed ahold of Jon's head and immediately pulled him forward. He shoved the entire length of his dick into Jon's mouth.

"Hey, man! This dick is a little fatter than Gary's was, isn't it. Kind of fits in your mouth a little tighter, don't it man?" Shawn asked.

Jon attempted to kind of shake his head in a 'Yes' motion, but was pretty well confined to just holding as completely still as possible so that Shawn could fuck him rather royally!

Shawn was not as patient with Jon as Gary had been. Jon decided that since he was the number two guy, that he could expect

Jon to know more of what to do and how to react to different things. He fucked Jon's face madly! He had no compassion for Jon being a beginner at this. He had Jon's mouth and he was anxious to really use it to his advantage!

"Hey, Wes!" Shawn said, in the direction of where Gary and Wes were now playing with each other. "Hey, Wes. This man is not getting as excited about doing my dick as I think would be nice, so I really do think that what maybe we should do, is get some of that grease out of my backpack over there, and give his ass some attention just like his mouth is getting. Wes, get some grease on your fingers and put one up in our man's asshole!"

Jon attempted to kind of yell, "No!" But to no avail!

Wes greased up his middle finger of his left hand, and after rubbing some grease around the outside of Jon's asshole, he inserted his finger up into the nice warm chamber.

Jon again attempted another "No!"

Again he attempted another indication that he did not want Wes's finger up in his ass, but each time that he attempted to utter any objection, Shawn would just slam his dick father down his throat so that he simply could not say anything at all.

"A dick in your mouth and a finger up in your ass! You are living man, you are living!" Shawn exclaimed! "Jon, my man. Do you know how many guys love to have two men in them somewhere at the same time? Man you are really getting treated right man! In your mouth and in your ass! Shit man! It's been too long since I've had that type of treatment!"

Shawn continued to fuck Jon's face, and Wes continued to play with his ass. As Shawn fucked, he continued to give Wes instructions as to what he wanted Wes to do with Jon's ass.

As the fucking got hotter and hotter, Shawn started yelling that he was about to cum, and he was forceful in his wanting Wes to have at least four of his fingers up in Jon's ass before he shot his load down his throat.

Once he got a confirmation that Wes had four fingers up in Jon's ass, and with much attempted distress from Jon, he then told Wes, "Keep them there, I am going to shoot off!"

Within just a few strokes, Shawn started throwing his head up in the air, and back and forth, and everybody else that was in the room knew he was right on the very edge of letting his cum load fly.

"Get ready Jon!" Gray said. "Shawn is getting really, really close! I can tell! He is about to let it blow! He is about ready to explode out of his dick, man! You are about ready to get another load and I'll bet it will be bigger than the one I fed you! Breathe through your nose! Get ready – get ready Jon! He's right there man – he's right there man – he's right there!"

Suddenly Shawn's body went completely still and rigid! Every muscle tightened up. He thrust his dick out in front and as far down Jon's throat as he could. He let out four very loud and strong moans. He jerked. He grabbed Jon's head and pulled him up tight to his body! Jon pushed back in an attempt to get his mouth off of the explosive dick.

Jon choked and coughed! He bent over and attempted to spit out some of the cum. It dripped from his mouth and his chin. He coughed again! He again attempted to spit out some of his mouth full! Wes pulled his fingers out of Jon's ass.

"Here man!" Gary said as he handed him another paper towel.

Jon took the towel and wiped his face and mouth, and then attempted to wipe part of the inside of his mouth.

Jon exclaimed. "Oh, shit, man! Let me rinse my mouth out again, please!"

Jon rinsed his mouth out and took a number of deep breaths.

"God, I'm trying for you guys, but shit, man! Damn, when you load my mouth all that full, I can't breath! God men! Is there a way to fuck me without shutting off my air supply?"

All three of the top fuckers looked at Jon when he asked that question!

"Oh, so getting face fucked isn't so bad after all, is that what I hear?" Asked Shawn. "Is there a way to fuck me without shutting off my air supply?" Shawn repeated.

"Hey, men! Sounds to me like getting face fucked is now kinda OK, but the lack of breath is kind of a problem. Is that what you're saying, Jon? Sounds to me like maybe the face fucking stuff has all of a sudden turned kind of OK. Right?"

"No, no!" Jon replied. No it is not! But I am smart enough to know there are three of you guys, all much younger than I am, all much stronger than I am, and I am not dumb enough to think that I can get out of here safely without doing whatever you three decide I am going to do, so all I'm saying is, I can't breath when you have your dick in my mouth and you are loading me up with sticky cum. That's what I am saying!"

"OK, so we make sure you are breathing!" Shawn answered – but not answered very seriously. "So how did Wes's fingers feel up in your butt, while I was fucking your face? Like that? Feel good man?"

"Hey!" Jon replied. "Like I just told you guys. I'm smart enough to know that to get the hell out of here all in one piece and get no bodily damage, that I would have to explain to either my wife and the kids, or even to the cops, that I'll just have to accept whatever, and no, the fingers up the ass did not feel good, but – like I said – whatever! Just got to just get this all over with and still be OK! Right now, that is my objective! And another objective is – to ask for some simple compassion as far as that damn big rod of that guy's! My God! That damn thing is way too big for any guy, of any size, to have hanging from his crotch!"

Jon was of course referring to Wes's dick, which he knew was next in line, and he knew he had to take as much of it as he could.

Once the small talk, or the getting things re-organized had happened, the three agreed that it was time to get things started again.

Agreeing with Gary's suggestion that Jon had expressed his understanding that he had no other choice than to just cooperate if he wanted out of this situation with no body harm, they decided to remove the ankle restrains so that Jon would have better body movement capabilities, especially since it was now Wes's turn to take care of him. All three agreed that Jon would need to use every available capability, available to him to take Wes successfully.

Once again they positioned Jon on the floor on his knees.

"Hey, guys!" Jon said. "Hey, guys I kind of think you guys have found out that if I try, then I can do your dicks, but since I have really tried to not be too much trouble, even though I do consider this whole thing as being gang raped, can we take it real slow with this guy so that I can kind of take it at my own pace?"

"Well, that's totally up to Wes!" Shawn answered. "It is now Wes's turn and it is up to him if he wants to take it slow or if he wants to see just how fast he can teach you to take about ten inches. Wes – what's your answer, man?"

"I think slow, at least at first is our best bet!" Wes replied. "Once I get it in him, then we will see. I like the way he has tried to do what we ordered, and I really do want to know that I was successful in getting my dick all the way in his throat, so at first, I think we will go slow, and then if he wants faster, I'm sure he will tell me, right Jon?"

Jon looked at Wes and replied. "Yeah! Yeah, if – and I do mean if – I can get that damn big thing down my throat! Men, shit men, this is really something for me. Shit men! I've already taken two big dicks down the throat and a big load from each of you guys! When guys get a dick in the mouth for the first time, do they usually get this much? I mean – men – you guys have pretty well worked me over for being my first time!"

Shawn looked at Gary, then looked at Wes and exclaimed, "For my first time!?"

"Men" he continued, "Did you hear that? Our toy boy is now referring to it as his first time. To me that kind of sounds like there will be additional times, right? So – hey maybe – just maybe, we have ourselves a new member of the, fuck my face group, that we can use! Sound like that to you, guys?"

The other two men shook their head and agreed.

"Well – wait a minute guys!" Jon exclaimed. "Wait! I did not mean that I'd ever do this again, but I just meant I had never done it before!"

"Yeah! Yeah – right!" Wes said. "Yeah – right! You haven't had me, yet! Just wait until you get this premium meat sick first, before you declare if you will ever, again or not. You've go to get the good stuff first – before you decide. Come on man, let me give you the Grade A meat, and then you decide."

Wes had a ragging hard-on! He had been excited during the previous two face fuckings and cum loadings, so he was anxious to get his chance. He walked up to the face of Jon, nicely positioned right at the right height for his entry, and said, "Open man. I need your mouth. Open wide! It's a big one!"

Jon did have to agree, at least to himself since he could not talk to anybody else, that yes – this sure as hell was a big one. He forced his mouth open as far as possible to get as much of Wes's dick in as he could.

Jon did seem to be much more into taking this dick than he had been on the two previous ones. He had been aware of this stick of meat ever since earlier, when he turned to look at it, and he decided that if he was going to be fed all three dicks, then he would go for as much enjoyment as possible on this one.

Wes was very experienced in knowing that he needed to be very patient with guys that had enough guts to even attempt to swallow his dick, so he did not force Jon into any situations that did not seem to work for both men.

Wes and Jon worked on Wes's dick very patiently and with great concern for their efforts. Slowly Jon managed to take more and more of Wes's dick, and Wes was well aware that he was being successful in getting it down Jon's throat.

"Man, you are doing good!" Wes complemented. "You are doing good!"

Shawn was feeling rather left out of the activity, especially since the actions were not as fast and ferocious as he personally preferred. He started fingering Jon's asshole.

As Shawn fingered Jon's ass hole, he reached over toward Gary and motioned for him to come closer. Gary approached. Shawn grabbed ahold of Gary's dick and started sucking on it. Now, things had developed into a four way. Jon was sucking on Wes, Jon was getting fingered by Shawn, and Shawn was also sucking on Gary's dick!

Jon had noticed what was happening, pulled off of Wes for a moment and commented, "Hey, guys! If we gotta do this, this is the way! All of us are involved, all at the same time! This is better man, it's better! I'm not the only one getting played with! Oh, shit, man! Oh, somebody's got their fingers up in my ass! Oh, man, that feels funny, but yeah, I'll admit, I kinda like it this time. Yeah, yeah, that feels kinda good!"

Nobody responded. Each man had his own personal agenda to attend to.

When Shawn heard Jon's positive comment about having his finger up in his asshole, he was very pleasantly surprised and increased his finger activity in Jon's ass. Jon responded positively and attempted to express his pleasure, but had a very large item rammed down his throat at the time, and that rather limited his abilities of responding.

Gary was now being sucked on by Shawn, as Shawn continued his fingering of Jon's ass, and Gary decided that Wes's ass just might be a little hungry too.

Jon knew that he was not the only person getting fingered in the ass, and he attempted to reach either Gary's ass or Shawn's ass since he was feeling left out of the ass actions, but both men were beyond his reach.

Gary saw Jon's actions, and accordingly told Jon, "Hey, man. For some virgin guy, you already have your mouth completely full, and now Shawn has got at least one finger up in your ass playing around, so I think you have got just about enough on your plate, so to say. You suck on that dick you got in your mouth, man! Wes is smiling one hell of a big smile, so you must be making him feel really good, so you just keep your mouth action going and make our man, Wes, feel really good, OK?"

Jon attempted to shake his head in a "yes" motion, but was restricted from doing too much up and down action. He was limited to an 'on and off' motion. And he was realizing how much longer the 'on and off' motion on this dick was, as compared to the two previous dicks.

Suddenly Jon felt somebody going onto his own dick. He managed to look down as far as he could and he realized that Gary was now sucking on his dick. Jon was in an almost complete shock. He was sucking on Wes's enormous dick, he was getting fingered in the ass by Shawn, and now he was getting sucked on my Gary. All three men were doing something to Jon, all at he same time. And each action was exciting!

Jon started some very fast and ferrous action on Wes's dick, which made his own dick get much more active in Gary's mouth, and of course his butt hole was getting more and more action down there as his other actions increased in speed and velocity.

Wes exclaimed. "Oh, Jon, suck me hard man! Suck me, man! Suck me! Oh, God guys, he has got my big rod all the way down his throat! Shit I can't believe this! Gary – Shawn – this guy has got all of me! Oh, Jon, suck me, man! Suck me!"

None of the other two could respond, since Gary had Jon's dick in his mouth, and Shawn was sucking on Gary's shaft! The only person without a dick in his mouth at that time was Wes.

All four men were in radical action. Fast and ferrous! Rough and ready! Wes was fucking Jon's face now as hard as he could. He continued to exclaim, "Oh, God men! I can't believe he has my whole dick! Guys he is a great sucker! Men, we need to keep him around. I need this guy on me a lot!"

Suddenly Jon was pushing his dick into Gary's face as far as possible and he pulled off of Wes's dick long enough to announce, "Oh, God men! I'm going to cum! I'm going to cum!"

Gary pulled off of Jon's dick and quickly almost screamed, "Good, good! Fill my mouth you – married – straight – daddy guy! I need some married daddy cum! Fill me daddy!"

He immediately grabbed Jon's dick and started feverishly sucking on it!

Shawn then pulled off of Gary's dick and instructed, "Fill my mouth Gary! Fill my mouth!"

All four men were completely engrossed in some very active and exciting sexual activity. All four men were active in one sex act or possibly two at the same time.

"Suddenly Wes said, "Jon suck me, man! Suck me hard man! I am gonna cum! Oh, Jon! I'm gonna cum! Suck me! Suck me! Oh,

God – here it comes! I'm cumin, I'm cummmmin! Oh, Jon – eat it man! Eat my cum man! Eat it man! Eat it – eat it – eat it! Yeah, eat it!!"

Immediately all four men climaxed at the same time, all in response to Wes's loud proclaimed cumin statements.

Jon shot his hot load into Gary's anxious mouth, Shawn had been stroking his own dick as he sucked on Gary and fingered Jon's ass. Gary let a solid stream of cum fly into Shawn's mouth as Wes was exclaiming his successful climax in Jon's mouth.

Jon was the one person that was supposed to be getting a mouthful, but things just did not quite work out that way! Jon got a mouth full, and Gary got a mouthful as a gift from Jon. Shawn got his loading directly from Gary! Wes was the only person in the room that did not have cum flowing from around his mouth. The other three men all had cum dripping out of the corners of their mouths!

As the four men managed to come to a pleasant halt of their activities, Shawn did say, "Well hell men! If I could have gotten my dick up high enough to get it in Wes's mouth, the whole group of us would be dripping with cum! I just could not get my dick up that high! Maybe we should have figured out ahead of time that all of us were going to be involved this time, and gotten ourselves in a different position!"

"Shit man!" Gary exclaimed. "Who in the hell thought that was going to happen. Man, that was great, but who in the hell would have thought that all four of us were going to be having one big sex scene? I guess our man Jon, is kind of a joiner, wouldn't you guys?"

"Hey, wait a minute men!" Jon quickly entered. "Hey, let's not get everything all confused here men. Yeah, yeah – I will agree that I kind of got into what was happening here, but that was only after I decided that I could not get away from you three husky younger guys, and that I had better just play along if I wanted to be OK. Just because I did what you wanted, don't lead that to think that I'd do this again. You guys can't seem to remember I am a married straight guy, and I am a daddy too. Hey, guys, what happened here has to be completely our secret. Yeah, I do know that I could create a lot of problems for all of you and call the law – I mean – let's face it, you three actually raped me, and on public property no less. I hear possible jail! No, I'm not going to do anything. Nobody got hurt. Yeah, I admit I got forced into doing some stuff that I did not want to do, but I can live and let live. Just don't think that I'd be willing to join in again, OK?"

"Yeah!" Gary answered. "OK guys, Wes, Shawn, we understand he got trapped and was forced into this and – right – we don't expect him to do it again with us, right? Hey, men – better agree! He is right! He could call the cops! He could get all of us in a ton of trouble. Better tell him that yeah, we all understand and won't expect him to do it again, even if we happen to be here at the same time he is. OK?"

"Yeah, you are right!" Shawn said. "Yeah, Jon. I understand! Thanks for not getting the cops after us man! But hey Jon. I've got to tell you though – you were fun! I really had fun with you!"

"Thanks man! I'm glad you enjoyed it! It's not my bag, but I'm glad you enjoyed it!"

"Yeah, me too." Wes said. "I mean, yeah I agree. You are right Jon. Thanks for letting us have some fun, but yeah I understand that this is not your bag and I will not try anything with you in the future. Yeah – you were fun! And, man! How in the hell could you take my dick all the way like you did? Hell, I can't get some of my regular suckers to get it down their throat as far as you did. Shit man! You really do need to become a professional cock sucker!"

"Hey, Wes, thanks for the – complement – I guess! I mean to be called a good cock sucker is not exactly what I've always looked forward to being called, but it's better than some of the stuff I've been called before. Wes, you do have a big dick! I guess my time on it was what they call beginners luck!"

"You know what men?" Gary asked. "It kind of looks like all of us have a little bit of washing up to do to be presentable. Let's get cleaned up. Jon, where do you live? Do you want me to drive you to your neighborhood and drop you off someplace close to your house, since we've taken a lot of your time? I'm sure your wife or the kids will ask you why you are so late, if you just resume your run. Want me to drop you off so you don't get home too late?"

"Yeah, Gary, yeah! I really would appreciate that! Maybe we should have discussed this before we got started. My getting home too late has been a real concern to me during this whole thing. Yeah, Gary, I live over by Maple and 4th Ave. If you could, that really would be a great help. I really don't want to have to explain any of this to the family! Yeah, thanks Gary, I'd really appreciate that!"

The men tidied themselves up, and after checking each other to make sure nobody was leaving the restroom with cum stuck to his face, they headed for the parking lot.

Each of the men, except for Jon, had his own car in the lot. Gary told Jon which car was his and they headed for it.

Gary turned toward Shawn and Wes and said, "Hey, guys! Thanks for the fun. I'll see you guys tomorrow! OK?"

Both Shawn and Wes responded with a, "Yeah, man. See you tomorrow!"

Jon yelled, "Bye guys!"

Gary and Jon got in Gary's car. As they exited the parking lot, Gary looked at Jon and grinned. Jon returned the grin. For a moment neither man said anything!

Then as the left the park area, and entered the city street, Jon spoke. "Well – what do you think man? Think we pulled it off?"

Gary looked at Jon with a very, very, big grin on his face, and replied, "Hell yes man! Hell yes! Neither one of them has any idea, no idea – not even now – that this whole thing was a total set up!"

Jon grinned back and said, "I totally, totally agree! Neither one of them even acted like they suspected anything! They were totally, faked out! They thought they were raping me, they did! They thought I was getting face fucked and fingered up in my ass for the very first time! They thought they had a virgin mouth and a virgin ass! And man, I gotta agree with you – that dick on that Wes guy is one hell of a big dick, especially for on such a small guy! You sure were right about that thing! Hey, man – are we still gonna go to your place for awhile? I don't need to be home until about 8:30 or so. The wife and the kids are all out doing their things. I really do need to get another one of your good ole ass fuckings! And, if you feel like it – I sure am ready to eat out that ass of yours and fuck your tight little ole butt hole, again! I haven't had my mouth on that hole of yours for probably a week and a half, and making those guys think that they were raping the hell out of me, has really, really, gotten me all turned on fucking hot and heavy! I'm horny as hell for you and some hot fucking action, man! I need you! And I hope like hell you are ready to pound my ass like crazy! After that, I need it – I do!"

ABOUT THE AUTHOR

Wade is a senior citizen living in Arizona where he skipped out to, in about 1964, from a very bad winter in Ohio. Did not care for where he was living – did not care for his job, and the summer before, he and three friends drove from Ohio, to Seattle, to Tijuana, Mexico, to the Grand Canyon, Las Vegas and back home – and that showed him, that if you put your mind to it, you can do some pretty unexpected things!

Wade Wright is also the author of ***Yes, Cops Do It – Oh Yeah; The Two Straight Guys; Apartment 117; The Carpet Installer; Marshmallow Cream – and Hard Big Pieces of Chocolate; In Cemetery Park;*** and ***Jay, Jake and Jimmy;*** available from TheNazcaPlainsCorp.com, Amazon.com, or your local bookstore.

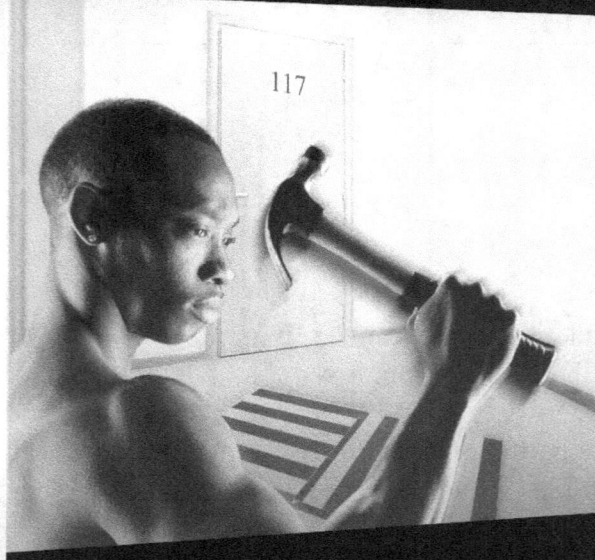

APARTMENT 117

117

a novel by
WADE WRIGHT

WRIGHT

APARTMENT 117

A
BONER
BOOK

JAY, JAKE AND JIMMY

A NOVEL BY

WADE WRIGHT

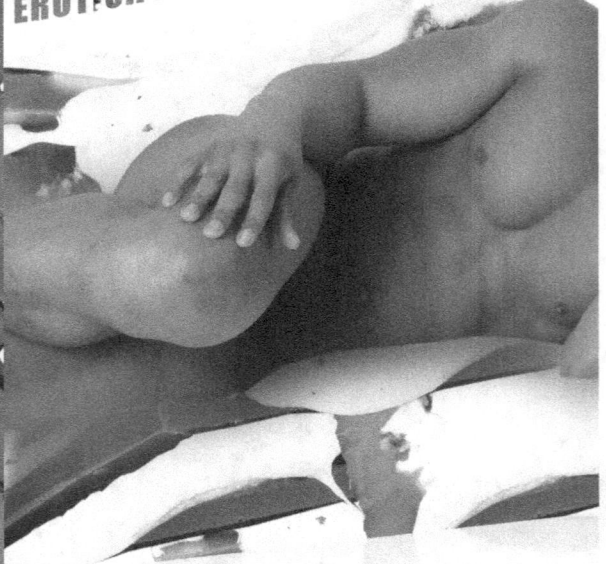

MARSHMALLOW CREAM
– AND HARD BIG PIECES OF CHOCOLATE

EROTICA BY WADE WRIGHT

A ROWEN BOOK

Wright

The Two
Straight
Guys

The Two Straight Guys

a novel by

Wade Wright

A
BONER
BOOK

"YES, COPS DO IT,
– OH YEAH!"
a collection of stories by
WADE WRIGHT
WRIGHT
"YES, COPS DO IT, – OH YEAH!"
A
BONER
BOOK

IN CEMETERY PARK

A NOVEL BY

WADE WRIGHT

IN CEMETERY PARK

The Carpet Installer

Wade Wright

A
BONER
BOOK